ONE NIGHT ONLY

ONE NIGHT ONLY

EROTIC ENCOUNTERS

EDITED BY
VIOLET BLUE

CLEiS
PRESS

Published in the United States by Cleis Press, Inc., 2246 Sixth Street, Berkeley, California 94710.

Printed in the United States.
Cover design: Scott Idleman/Blink
Cover photograph: B2M Productions/Getty Images
Text design: Frank Wiedemann
First Edition.
10 9 8 7 6 5 4 3 2 1

Trade paper ISBN: 978-1-57344-756-0
E-book ISBN: 978-1-57344-775-1

Contents

INTRODUCTION:
ONE CHANCE

*T*he train slid to a stop, the motion pressing a
nicely firm cock against my ass. I grinned, now
sure that I wasn't the only one getting all hot and
bothered. As the car began to move again, I shifted
my hips subtly to press a little harder against him,
using the swaying rhythm for extra oomph. I felt
one twitch of his cock, then another. I was feeling
pretty smug when I felt lips against the nape of my
neck and I stilled. He gave a swirl of his tongue at
the base and I moaned out loud. A puff of breath
against my skin let me know that he was amused,
which prompted me to resume my subtle lap dance.
His hand dropped to my hip, pulling me even tighter
against him, making me more aware of each movement while his lips continued to explore the back of
my neck. My heart was tripping; I was getting wetter
by the minute.

—"Subway Subterfuge," by May Deva

One chance to take what you want: that's all you get. I know you've done it at least once before.

A furtive make-out session in a movie theater—or parked car—that turned into a desperately quiet grope-and-grind session.

The stranger in a public café, park or bar who turned your dials and, miraculously, zeroed in on you, too: did you rut or suck like animals in the unisex restroom behind a locked door... or was that only in your mind?

Did you ever sneak a silent slice of mutual satisfaction under a table, or into your dorm when your roommates were sleeping mere feet away? What about playing "hall pass" with your sweetie so that you could feel the thrill of his basest need to use you, in a car park, in a filthy side alley, or on crisp hotel sheets usually reserved for specialty escorts?

It's okay—you don't need to have acted on your naughty impulses. This book, and all its nervous, adventurous, realistic and frolic-minded characters do it all for your entertainment and inspiration. Of course, if you have tried out a one-night, one-time tryst, the satisfied characters in this collection will have you feeling in pleasant, heady, and familiar company.

One Night Only is a compendium of the most refined zipless fuck fantasies imaginable. Even if you've only ever longed for a one-night stand, a quickie with a hot and dominant customer at work, getting your hands and mouth on a longtime crush, or picking up a little side action while indulging in a mistaken identity opportunity...it's all here to feed your wildest fantasies and stoke embers in your hottest memories of one-time fantasy fulfillment. The stories here are about women and men (and couples) who are erotic chance-takers, each and every one of them—and all of them emerge deliciously satisfied.

"Seeing Stars," by Alison Tyler, begins our adventures with a girl who works at a popcorn stand in a revival movie house and studies astronomy. Over-the-counter nervous flirtation leads to a sexy stranger promising to show her the stars—and she takes him up on what turns out to be a heated, romantic offer.

In "Chasing Fate: Exige," by Kev Henley, a sexy car thief is zooming around in a stolen Lotus when he spots a hot girl he knew in high school (a year or two previously). She jumps in—they race, flirt, and do it on the hood when neither can take the tension any longer. Emerald's "City Girl," goes back home to the Midwest to a county fair. To her surprise, she sees a hot cowboy, and cruises him, sneaking off for a surprising fantasy fuck.

May Deva's "Subway Subterfuge" tells of a young woman attracted to a hot guy on the subway; they move to the back of the crowded car where we find out she's the one driving the anonymous public encounter. "Performance Art," by Cynthia Hamilton, gives public sex an unexpected twist. A tourist in France gets turned on at an exhibit of erotic installations. A male tourist has the same reaction, and what happens next for the unsuspecting art patrons is equal parts arousing, shocking and even a little bit adorable.

"Let Sleeping Dogs Come" involves a chance meeting at a book expo that ends with a surprise oral encounter. At an upscale hotel, a slacker provides some very wicked "Maid Service"; author Jan Darby offers an empowering revision of recent headline events. Another sort of accommodation is provided by a woman with a longtime secret attraction when her old college crush crashes at her apartment, in Donna George Storey's "Hole in Your Pocket."

Trendy food trucks never looked as tasty or satisfying as the one in "Chasing Jared," by Heidi Champa; she's a fan of the burgers and the chef making them, and one late night she tracks the truck down, goes inside, and before she gets her burger, decides to order off-menu. The college girl in "Breathing," by Daniel Burnell, silently dares the fear of getting caught when she passes out on a basement couch at a party and wakes up to sneak mutual satisfaction with a shy guy pal from drama class in a dark room full of people, all without words.

The best thing about each of these stories, besides the hot sex and great writing, is the thrill of the unplanned—and "Whore" by D. L. King does not disappoint. In it, a neurosurgeon with a sexy new dress stays over an extra night after a boring conference only to get picked up by a distinguished older guy in the hotel bar for a truly smutty coupling, with a twist that befits the story's title. In another city and another world, Austin Stevens's "Belle de Soir" follows a young woman who goes to work as a high-class hooker for just two days with the plan of heading for Europe on the money she'll make, not expecting to get more than the needs of her pocketbook met.

Sexy fun at the trendy punk salon is what we find in "Just a Little Trim" by Kristina Wright. A hot former Marine comes in for a trim, and we find ourselves surprised at what a clever, horny hairdresser can do with a minimum of time and cover at the shampoo station.

Truly outrageous public sex on a whim revs up in "Three Pink Earthquakes" by Thomas S. Roche. This San Francisco story will have natives wondering how much is true in this narrative of a woman getting sleazy under a table with an Italian tourist couple—first the woman, then her husband, in a Castro gay bar. More turnabout happens in "The Spoiled Brat," by Lily K. Cho; in it, a recently divorced woman goes out to celebrate her lesbian sister's birthday at a gay bar when a gay male couple invite her to dance and ask her home with them.

The most edgy, intense story in this collection is "An Audience of One," by N. T. Morley, in which a Hollywood B-actress gets to live her most extreme sexual fantasy just once, all arranged by her boyfriend, and including a deserted scary neighborhood and faux-forced-group-sex. Staying on the edge, "Chocolate Cake," by I. G. Frederick, finds us with a woman who, at home, is a Domme to two submissive males yet lets herself be picked up while traveling by a hot dominant guy, for a change of pace.

"Tournament," by Abby Abbot, is the most unpredictable story in the lot; here, a college girl plays online chess and she's out for both blood and money when she agrees to an in-person match. The meeting and the match feel tense and dangerous and finish with an unusual, frenzied erotic battle. Rachel Kramer Bussel's "Rock Star Rewards" tells of a famous female rock star with an appetite for hot but submissive male groupies.

Passion and lust play by different rules in *One Night Only*; these are stories about what happens when we have just that one chance to ask for what we want—and we take it. If you're looking for instant gratification sex and a catalog of encounters that show what happens when we need it *now*, you'll find your thirst for unplanned new experiences quenched in these pages.

Just because you're all grown up doesn't mean you can't enjoy the thrill of sex without a plan. Enjoy the adventure. You have one night and *One Night Only*.

Violet Blue
San Francisco

SEEING STARS

Alison Tyler

I have that morning-after look.

The morning after the night before.

My tortured curls are misbehaving. My dark eyes are ringed in yesterday's kohl, which looked so sexy around nine p.m. but is raccoon-inspired this a.m. My clothes are—well, my clothes are pretty much what my clothes are always: jeans and a T-shirt, Docs and leather wristbands, a thrift-store Edie Sedgwick sweatshirt shrunk a few sizes too small so that it fits. I mean, *really* fits. What's different about me is that I'm up. The sun's peeking out, and I'm awake—two facts that usually do not occur simultaneously. See, I work nights at a retro theater in L.A.—nights, meaning, I get off around two. That's not the only place I work, but it was where I was working last night, when he walked in.

You've heard the clichés: The bells. The whistles. The flashes of bright light. Our connection was different. The popcorn began overflowing the stainless steel kettle, startling me even though I *am* the popcorn girl around here. I ought to know how to deal with the familiar sounds of tiny explosions ricocheting off the glass.

But I'm getting ahead of myself. Or behind. I go to school, hit the books, work the popcorn shift. I study in between movies—most of the demand for popcorn comes before the show starts and at intermission, which gives me plenty of time to do my coursework. Last night, my head was in the stars. Literally. I'd been studying for my astronomy final. But I was prepping for the intermission rush and he appeared at first pop.

Sounds like a song from the fifties, doesn't it?

He was dressed in a fashion nearly identical to mine. "Adult still-in-school style," I call the look: black jeans, some leather and chrome hardware. I struggled to remember what double feature we were playing. The themes call out to different segments of the population. Was it *Sid & Nancy* and *Last Tango*? Or maybe…?

"Don't burn yourself."

He was right up at the glass by then, leaning on the counter, which is a no-no. There's a sign, handwritten by the owner. PLEASE DON'T LEAN ON THE GLASS. I didn't snap at him. I didn't point out the obvious. The popcorn kept thundering out of the kettle, and I felt my cheeks go as pink as a Good and Plenty.

What were the movies? A nice detective mystery? Something noir?

"Would you like popcorn?"

He shook his head.

"Candy?" I did the tried-and-true Vanna White move, motioning to the display of goodies with a spokesmodel gesture. I didn't have the hair flip down. Not with my tangled mane.

He smirked.

Damn, we really did look similar. He had dark hair, too.

Longish like mine. Big dark eyes. Was he wearing liner? Were we showing *Velvet Goldmine*? He was built slim, long limbed. His lips were almost pretty.

"Do you get tired of the smell of hot butter?"

I shook my head.

"Do you get tired of people asking you what you're reading?"

I nodded.

"What are you reading?"

I smiled. "Astronomy." I held up the text.

"You like stars?"

"When you can see them."

"How about tonight, after you get off?"

"How about tonight, after I get off, *what*?" Except I knew. I knew exactly what. It was put your lips together and blow time, wasn't it?

"We go look at some stars."

"I've never heard fucking called that before," I said, thankfully finding my moxie somewhere deep in my 501s.

"No, really," he said. "I've got a roof in mind."

I had something else in mind. I felt that connection, the way he looked at me. And it had been slow lately—the romance in my life. Not that there hadn't been comers, but there hadn't been anyone pushing my buttons the way I need them pushed.

"You can't see stars in L.A.," I said after a moment. I wasn't going to roll over that easily. "The sky's too bright."

"Try me."

I gazed at him. This man had a look I liked. Oh, I'm no narcissist. I don't mean that I liked him because he looked like me. He had an underlying quality that made me think I could ask for anything and he'd give me what I wanted: A little dirty around the edges. A little beat-in. Besides, my kernels hadn't been popped for quite a while.

"Theater closes around two tonight," I said. "Are you game for hanging out?"

He brandished half of the torn paper ticket. "I bought the ticket," he said, "I'll ride the ride."

Studying didn't work much after that. I mean, I didn't work much at studying. All I could think of was the way he'd looked at me from across the lobby. The way my knees had gone instantly weak, my pussy immediately wet. I handed out popcorn at the intermission. I made change. I poured sodas. I dug the metal shovel into the crushed ice. But my mind was on the man. I even considered ducking into the ladies' room to rub one out. Just so I wouldn't be such a bundle of nerves when the movie's *fin* finally came. But I couldn't. Couldn't leave my post, couldn't imagine leaning up against the tiled wall and touching myself—well, that's not true. *That* I could imagine. But somehow, I felt I'd be cheating. Cheating him, cheating me.

He wanted to show me the stars. In a city where all you have to do to see one is know which supermarket to visit, which hair salon to book a cut at, which bar to dive in. I couldn't remember a more romantic proposition.

When the movie ended, I did all the closing-down things I do every weekend night. Made sure the popper was off. Locked the cash box in the owner's office; said good night to the projectionist. I went outside, and there he was, waiting.

"Do you have a car?"

I nodded. "But it's not here. I live within walking distance." I motioned, vaguely, toward Melrose.

"You'll go with me?"

"You'll take me home after?"

We smiled at each other—silent answers to spoken questions. The *after* was my way of saying yes before he'd even propositioned me, wasn't it? The *after* told us both all we needed to know.

In L.A., in a land of high-end vehicles that are lovingly washed more often and more carefully than most people's own children, this man drove a pickup truck. Not a tricked-up, monster-tired showcase, either, but an old, rust-colored Chevy that looked as if its parts were held together with twine. He held the door for me, and I slid in. There were peanut shells on the floor. Gum wrappers in the ashtray from Doublemint. My favorite.

He drove me into the hills, to one of those vintage apartments where the extras used to live when Hollywood made the type of movies we show at our theater: wrought iron railing on the balconies, the kinds of details missing from today's stucco nightmares. The place wasn't well kept—in fact, it was a lot like his truck, a lot like himself. Good lines, but smudged around the edges.

He didn't take me inside. He grabbed an old army blanket from the bed of the truck and then took me up the back stairs. To the roof. Nine floors up.

To the stars.

We were already in the Hollywood foothills, and now we were up on the rooftop, and I could see a few lone stars twinkling overhead.

But I didn't care about the stars anymore. He spread out the blanket. He spread me out on the blanket. I let him. I let him peel off my sweatshirt, my T-shirt, my bra; felt him work the ties of my Docs, pull off my stripy socks, demolish my white knickers, kill the jeans. I was naked and he was dressed, and the stars were above us, the way the stars always are.

He took my hands and put them over my eyes.

"I thought you wanted me to look at the stars," I said. Smart-ass: that's me.

"I do," he said. "You'll see them. Trust me."

My hands smelled like popcorn and licorice whips. I kept my eyes closed even under my fingers. I felt him moving on the blanket, felt him parting my thighs, getting in between. He kissed the insides of my legs, nipping gently. I groaned and arched, hips moving against that scratchy, khaki-colored blanket. Army surplus: I had one in the back of my own beat-up hoopdee truck. It's like they come regulation with trucks like ours.

We were nine floors up, but we were on top of the world, on top of Los Angeles. His mouth crested over my pussy, not locking on, not licking in. He was teasing me. I was shuddering.

School takes most of my time. I'm not going to be a popcorn girl forever, you know. But this—I'd forgotten about this. Bliss. That white-hot connection you get once in a double feature, that's once in a long time coming.

He moved his way down, kissing along my thighs, moving lower and lower, to the backs of my knees, my calves. I kept my hands over my eyes. But I peeked. I opened my eyes and looked through my fingers. He seemed to know exactly when I did, because he said, "No cheating. Close your eyes." How had he guessed? Had I shifted on the rough blanket, crunching the tiny rocks beneath me? Had I breathed in deeper? I pushed the questions from my head and let myself float in the way he was making me feel: weightless. That's the first thing I noticed. As if I were flying on a magic carpet rather than an old army surplus blanket. He touched and stroked his way back up my body, not stopping in the middle this time, going higher, cradling my breasts, kissing and nipping. He reached my mouth and I was ready for him, hungry for him. I realized that I liked the way he felt—clothes on to my clothes off. I wasn't cold. That surprised me. I'm always cold. But he warmed me with his body on mine, his lips on mine. As he kissed me, really kissed me, he worked one hand between our bodies. I felt what he was doing, ached for what he was doing.

He was out, against me, I could feel how hard and ready he was. Then he sat back, and I heard the rustle, the tear, knew he was putting on a condom. I wanted to peek once more, but I forced myself to keep still, be good.

He got back into position, and I felt the head of his cock nudge my pussy lips apart, felt him slide inside. There was nothing to compare to this. There never is. All I can says is...

"I needed this," he sighed, his mouth against my neck. "Oh, fuck, I needed to be in you as soon as I saw you."

Exactly that. Exactly what he said. It had been too long. Way too long. I'd forgotten what sex was for, what sex can do. A connection—a raw, powerful connection—that can make you feel...

"Look," he said, "take your hands away and look."

I stared up at the sky. There weren't stars. Not like you can see outside of the city. Not like you could see in my book. It was just night in L.A., too polluted and too well lit to see much of anything. There were dozens, not millions, but beautiful nonetheless. You forget to look up in a city like this. You forget to take your eyes off the road.

Did I feel let down? Did I feel...

"Close your eyes again."

I did, shut them tight, and he fucked me. Fucked me so hard, the way I always need it, the way I crave being taken. He ground into me, thrust his cock so deep to fill me up. I groaned and bucked, realizing I didn't have to lie still, I could move with him, I could help him. Our bodies were linked—that magic crazy heat we'd felt back in the movie theater lobby had never left us. Together we burned twice as hot.

And then he crested his thumb up and over my clit, and I

shuddered. He was taking me closer, faster. Behind my clenched lids, I saw glimmers of light. Seeing stars: was this what he'd meant? I didn't care that we were in the city—that the black velvet skies shown in my book didn't exist here, that the only stars you could be secure in seeing paraded down Rodeo Drive. I bit my lip, I felt him touch me again, and came.

Seeing stars. That's what he'd called it. I understood. The power flooded through me, and back to him, and he came a beat after, as if riding the comet tail of my pleasure. Behind my shut lids, I saw ricochets of light, explosions of color. I bit my bottom lip and let the pleasure swirl through me. I waited for him to tell me when to open my eyes, but he didn't.

Instead, he lay down at my side. He pulled the blanket over me. He turned me to face him. Without being told, I opened my eyes. Fuck the stars, I'd rather stare into his eyes any dawn of the week.

He pressed his lips to mine. I pressed mine back. Kissing was good like this, where I could taste myself on his lips, taste the way we melted. We lay tangled in the blanket together, one of his jeans-clad legs over mine, sealed tight in an army surplus envelope. We stayed like that until the chill seeped in. Until I needed to slip my clothes back on, and he folded the khaki surplus into a tight rectangle; watched while I fastened up my laces, shook out my hair. We walked nine flights down holding hands. Nine flights in silence—quiet like the stars hidden overhead. He drove me home on nearly empty streets. I love Los Angeles before the city wakes up. On my direction, he drove me to my triplex bungalow where my nearly identical truck was parked in the drive. He chuckled when he saw the Chevy. Mine was rusted brown instead of rusted orange.

He kissed me again with his engine running. "You still smell of popcorn," he said into my hair.

"Always," I told him as I breathed him in. "You smell of the night air," I said, "and stars over Los Angeles." Stars I hadn't believed in until he'd shown me a different way to look.

I creaked open the door, crushed shells underfoot as I got out. I walked to my front door without a look behind. I could feel him watching. That was enough.

Today I'll sleep well. Until the stars come out again.

CHASING FATE:
EXIGE

Kev Henley

Ah, listen to that purr! A red light catches me—RPMs leap into the red as she growls and rolls to a stop. It's a balmy night, and excitement stirs the breeze. Neon colors bounce off the deep blue curves of the Lotus Exige. *Tired of stealing SUVs and shit. This car has soul.*

People stare at sexiness fused with speed. *And right now I'm king behind the wheel.*

What's this? Little gangbanger looking to get owned? Too much bass beat and not enough class in your made-over Civic. Sucks to be you—you're on!

Green light.

Ease through the first five miles-per-hour while the lil' puke fishtails. Punching it unleashes the supercharged 220 horses. The Lotus leaps forward, riding her traction threshold. *Breathe. Shift. Out. Tick, tick, shift. Four seconds to sixty hasn't felt this good since racing school. Eat shit, motherfucker! Cya!*

Other cars are colored blocks of garbage, obstacles to give a good time. *Brake. Control the sliding turn. Recover.*

"Woo!" *She loves her new master—whoa, Kate!* The Lotus throws me against the restraints as I decelerate and sweep against the curbside.

The passenger window slides down and I yell over the street noise. "Hey, Kate!" She sees the car before she sees me and steps toward the curb.

"Derrick? *Nice car!*" She leans in and checks out the sports-trimmed interior before focusing on me with a funny expression. If I were forced to be picky, I'd say she's a little short for my taste, but one hundred percent spunk. Lively, sassy eyes; a cute little nose over full lips; long brunette fluff held in check by a brightly colored hair clip. And a tight body built for speed fucking. We've teased, played around before, but nothing beyond longing.

"Only been a year since we graduated," she says, laughing in delight at my ride, at my boyish grin and flexed arms. "What have you been doing to earn this kind of life?"

"It's borrowed." I cock an eyebrow, inviting her to dare me. "Care to feel how she moves?"

She only needs one quick glance back at her girlfriends to make up her mind—the same boring Friday night out with her buds, or a spin in this. There really is no choice. She gets in, short skirt showing her own lithe curves. I wait for her to caress the trim, to adjust to the idea that she's sitting in a car as hot as she is before revving the engine and pulling back into the street. She waves good-bye to her girlfriends with an energetic *whoop* as I crawl up to the speed limit.

Always start them off slow for the first few seconds. "Hang on," I warn her the instant before I accelerate through a turn and around a rolling impediment.

"Yes! That kicks *ass*, Derrick." She says this even as she's braced hard against the seat, but never even thinks to put her seat belt on. She is *so* my type: thrill junkie to the core. "Now I'm beyond curious." She has to raise her voice against the combined wind and road noise, so I settle down into cruise speed and run up the windows.

"Ask away—no way can I refuse a beauty, as you can see." I motion to her but end up indicating the car, much to her amusement. She has a considering look when she continues.

"Been too long since I've seen you—what you been up to?"

"This and that." I smile at my evasiveness and wait for her to protest before continuing. "Actually, I collect cars for my cousin when not going to the U."

"And you 'collected' this sweet Lotus?" Had I been a lesser driver, I'd have wrecked from my shock.

"Okay, now I'm impressed! How'd you know it was a Lotus?"

"The logo, silly." She reaches over to tap the steering wheel. Had she not had that special glow, I'd have felt the fool. "I see you still hit the weights." She gives my biceps a squeeze, and I flex them—impossible not to when they receive this kind of attention.

"And I see you're still a sexy bundle of energy." No way was I going to let this stay one-sided. Throughout high school, we were both on the track team. Saturdays laying out on the midfield in between events were as memorable as the parties, in their own special way.

"Dancing as wildly as I do has its strengths." She deflects nicely, but it's not that easy.

"Only dancing, eh?" I load that with teasing doubt, and though she slaps my arm, she keeps her hand on me. *I'm going to get a taste of her sweet body.* I twitch in my blue jeans.

Life always tries to fuck with you—see what kind of stuff

you're made out of. Case in point, the cop car pulling onto the road behind me and hitting his lights. *Too early for them to have a clue, though my speed was maybe a hair over legal—no way am I running with her here.* That's why there's always a Plan B.

"Uh-oh," she intones when she sees the swirl of red and blue, removing her hand. Mr. Cop sits for a while, running the dealer plates I attached. I reach over to the glove box.

"Excuse the reach." I wink, removing the insurance card and my license. "Don't sweat it, Kate. There's nothing he can get me on, and we'll forget about him soon enough." I roll down my window, showing my hands and the documentation, which almost always speeds them up.

"Evenin', Officer. How can I help you?" I ask in a pleasant tone. Older piggy—*probably jealous as hell*—takes the insurance and license before peering at us in silence.

"Mr. Dane," he reads, "everything okay in here?" I look up in confusion to see he's eyeing Kate. *Oh! Chivalrous fucker—glad I didn't have to embarrass him.* "Ma'am, everything okay?"

"Who me?" She's as baffled as I was a moment ago. Harassing cops deserve to get beat, but those who make sure women are okay get a pass, in my book. Never hurts to be sure.

"He's asking if you're safe, Kate," I explain.

"Oh! Of course, Officer."

"You will be safer and *legal*," he stresses the word, "with your seat belt on."

"Oh, my god, sorry, Officer. Sorry." The cute, apologetic smile she flashes him as she reaches to put on her belt would get us out of any ticket.

"Nice car, Mr. Dane," he comments, handing back my paperwork.

"Thanks, Officer." Meaning, "thank you for the leniency."

"My uncle owns the dealership."

"Lucky you." The corner of his mouth twitches. "Well, keep it legal and have a good night."

"Yes, sir. We will."

"Very smooth," Kate comments as I roll the window back up and replace my insurance card in the glove box. "But you're a liar."

"Oh?" I arch an eyebrow at her, and her eyes sparkle.

"Said you worked for your cousin, and you told the cop it was your uncle."

"The dealership's his father's, which makes him my uncle, in case you slept through school." The playful slap was back, but she looked disappointed. "You seem let down."

She shrugged slightly. "I guess I expected a spicier story behind such an incredible car." *Hmm, should I?* I considered her for a few seconds before putting the Lotus in gear and pulling back out into traffic.

"So, maybe I'm just a good liar." I laugh at her gasp of mock offense. "If you're good, maybe I'll share a secret with you about this work of art."

After a moment: "How about if I let you fuck me on it?" She sets her hand on my thigh. *And there it is—booya!*

"For that dream-come-true, I'd definitely tell you. Just tell me when and where."

"How about the first place we won't be arrested?" *I just knew this night would be good!*

"You, dearest Kate, are my type of girl. A real shame we didn't know this earlier."

"As I recall, you were pounding my friend, and I don't do that to friends."

"Another thing I admire. You gotta stop there, or I'll fall for you." She rubs my leg faintly.

"You may be in trouble, then," she says with a smirk. She squeals in delight as I pull us through a sideways gee and into a parking lot blessed with deep shadows. She moves her hand upward to my bulge.

"No chance I can wait any longer."

"So I see." She squeezes me before getting out of the car. I meet her around the hood and crush her to me. Her kiss is frenzied as she kneads my back; her hands drop to my ass, pulling my bulge harder against her.

"God*damn*," I pant, pulling away for air, "you're a she-devil." Her hands fly to my crotch, and I spring free in less time than it takes the Lotus to get to sixty. She gives me a knowing grin as she pushes me back on the car and engulfs me. *Hey, it's not my paint job.*

After a momentary battle with her gag reflex, she reaches my pubes, and I swell as I feel moisture and heat near my balls. She pulls off with a gasp of breath and a happy expression before blowing cool night air on my twitching cock.

"You're so fucking hard," she praises me as she bunches up her skirt, showing light satin panties.

"Consider it a compliment to you," I counter, nearly out of breath. She turns, bending slightly and caressing her glowing white ass before moving the panties aside. The tan pucker and shiny, smooth lips greet me. *All-American pussy of the highest quality.*

I slide down the hood to align us as she grabs me, backing onto my powerfully swollen hard-on. I feel her heat, and she squeezes me tightly as she slips down onto me.

"Ugh," she grunts holding herself to me. "Love the way you fill me." Widening her stance, she rolls herself in small circles, and my tip knocks against her insides. She bucks, slides up and down a few times before exclaiming, "Fuck! I can't get the power I need." She comes up off me, panting with need, and pulls me up. "Pound me from behind."

She sticks her pert ass up at the fluorescent-lit night, and I see the gloss at the very top of her inner thighs. Moving her panties aside again, I enjoy the view as her pliant flesh swallows me.

"Derrick, goddamnit, fuck me hard!" Gripping her slim waist, I quickly ramp up to a hard yet rapid rhythm. She pushes back at me, growling encouragement, and I savor the compression of her muscles on me. The light's just good enough for me to see her anus pulse as she squeezes me, grunting with her efforts to find bliss. Just thinking about easing into the tight pucker sends me dangerously close.

The speed and effort take their toll, and she drops her head to the hood. Thinking she may collapse, I snake a supporting arm under her before resuming the hard strokes. She drops a hand back to massage us, to play with her clit, moaning at me with abandon. Her "ahs" ramp up, bouncing off the building wall.

"Hold in me," she pants. "Coming!" Her insides flutter as I bury in her and hold. Her hand knocks against my forearm, furiously. *This minx is frigging herself through an explosion.* Throwing her head back, hair flying, she nearly screams in time with her tremors. I stay one breath away from coming as she collapses; slipping out of her, I lower her gently until her knees touch the front of the hood.

"Awesome," she comments after that second's rest, kissing the Lotus before turning around to kneel before my glistening erection. Taking the head in her mouth, she quickly yanks my base. As her tongue swipes the underside of my head, I lose it. Gripping her free hand against my thigh, I arch and pulse come into her sucking mouth.

"Mmm," she moans, pulling off me with an audible *smack*, "what a treat! Now, let's drive until I get hot again."

"Look forward to it." With a shared smile of pleasure, we readjust our clothes and climb back into the sports car. I crack the windows to disperse the sex smells, and she laughs, leaning over to tongue my earlobe as I bring the Lotus back to life with a roar.

Distracted as I am, I almost miss the darkened police car creeping up the road. *Now is not the time to play nice.* The cop lights up as I jump onto the street, but I already have the momentum advantage as I slide around him, forcing him to brake and spin around.

Kate squeals as I jerk away from the pursuer and one glance assures me she matches my excitement. *I think I love this girl.*

"Some asswipe-not-minding-his-own-business must have called them. Time to focus." The engine screams before I yank into a turn and shift.

40 MPH.

Shift. Good riddance, speed limit.

55, 65.

Brake hard. Wait for it... Downshift. Turn. Accelerate. Brake. Turn. Thank god for good tires.

"The cop had no chance." I grin to see her breathless and flushed. "Almost as good as a fuck, isn't it?" She nods, watching everything at once. "In the glove compartment, you'll find several garage door openers." *Let's see... the Nob Hill to SOMA jump will give me enough time, but Pac is safer for her.* "Get out the one with a 4 on it. In eight blocks, we'll drop out of sight."

She is already fishing out the small devices and holding them up to see the numbers. "What then?" she asks as she finds the right one and replaces the others. I cut the lights and slow enough to cause no noise, not answering as I scan for signs of pursuit or someone watching.

"Punch it now." I instruct as I turn into the safe house. "We'll

get you away from me, make sure I'm clear, then get to a safe
area." I lurch to a stop, kill the engine, and turn to her. "Still
want to know my secrets?"

"Hell, yeah!" She makes me smile with pleasure at her attitude. *I do believe we'll be at it again in the near future.*

"As you've guessed, this car is hot. I've had considerable
driving training—far more than Average Joe Copper."

"So tell me something I don't know."

"You're incredibly beautiful when you're excited." She
presses against me, biting my neck playfully before drawing me
into a passionate kiss.

"Glad you think so."

"Don't have much time before I have to get this work of art
to a safe place. Perhaps if I get your number we can talk more
later?" She drags up her small purse from the floorboard and
digs through it, handing me a card. "Secretary, eh?"

"For now," she answers, getting out when I do. "If you don't
call me, I'm gonna be pissed."

I laugh. "Kate, only way I'd not call you is if you told me you
hated me and never wanted to hear from me again. Wish we had
more time tonight…"

"I understand, really. You'll just make it up to me later. So,
what happens to her?" She drags her hand along the spoiler as
she walks to me.

"She'll go to a new owner far away—one willing to pay forty
or fifty grand. Now to get you home, I'll—"

"Don't worry about it—I'll call my friend to come get me."

"Ah, cool. Do me a favor of walking a few blocks before
calling, so—"

"Hold on," she interrupts. I wonder what she's doing until
she slips off her wet panties and hands them to me. "For luck."
Then she kisses me for that last brief moment of heaven before

turning. I will never forget the look of her ass moving away in that short denim skirt, and knowing her smooth pussy is bare.

I open my mobile and hit speed dial.

On the third ring: "Yo."

"Hey, coz, it's sunny."

"Excellent."

"Need a report from number four."

"As good as done." We stay in contact as he leads me in, away from the patrol reports. Her panties are good luck; even if the cops weren't busy with more important matters than a PDA runner, they'd have guided me home.

"You *dumb* fuck!" He shouts into my shit-eating grin as I get out of the Lotus. "No way can we off-load a unique car like this."

"It's a Lotus, coz—a work of art." *You ignoramus.*

"I don't give a fuck what brand it is." He kicks the tire in frustration. "They are all the 'Get-Fucked' brand as far as I'm concerned." *Funny—now that you mention it, I did get fucked on it.* But I sigh and proceed in a calming, rational voice.

"Cars disappear all the time to wealthy Mexicans; this one is no exception."

"*Bullshit*! Not with this price tag; they'll trace it."

"Umm, coz? This car costs sixty grand, loaded."

"Bullshit." But the wind is out of his psycho-righteous sail.

"Gone are the days you have to spend a hundred and fifty grand for a great ride."

"Hmm."

"Try it," I urge.

He growls and turns his back on me. "I'll think about it." He storms off, but I know that means he will and will like it. Eventually.

"Another thing," he pokes his head back around the corner.

"Don't fuck with my business again. I don't pay you to give me ulcers." *I really gotta take him with me next time.* I almost laugh; no doubt in my mind there will be a repeat. Maybe next time, I'll scale up.

Can't ever slow down, can I?

CITY GIRL

Emerald

Deep-fried cheesecake?" Isabel gestured at the vendor as we passed to prove she wasn't making the referenced item up. The food at the state fair was, of course, famous, and in the several years since I had been back to attend, the list of offered items had grown exponentially. My understanding was that the category of "deep-fried" in particular seemed to get more outrageous every year.

"I'm saving up for a funnel cake," I said, wrinkling my nose at the idea of cheesecake in deep-fried form. I scanned the food stands that stretched as far as we could see. I remembered funnel cake fondly as part of virtually every trip I'd made to the fair as a kid—a classic fair staple, the smell of which still instantly transported me back there any time I encountered it.

Spotting a stand nearby, I started to charge forward but was cut off by a family with a stroller crossing in front of me. I held up and waited as my body stood coiled, ready to move at the first opportunity. As soon as I began to advance through a clearing, a couple veered across my path, and I tapped my foot.

"What are you so impatient about?" Isabel said from behind me. "We're not in a hurry."

I stopped, feeling the adrenaline chasing through me as I stood consciously still. She was right. I stayed in one place until the automatic forward momentum I felt rushing through my system faded.

"I'm not used to the Midwest anymore," I said.

It was startling to realize how true it was. The rushed, impersonal environment I had grown used to for almost the last decade was simply missing here, and while I found it unnerving in a way, there was a place too where I experienced it as relieving—as well as undeniably familiar. I had grown up amongst the sedate, grounded undercurrent of the Midwest, unmistakable even here among the energy and extravagance of the state fair.

In the nine years since I'd moved away, I'd been back at least once each year for Christmas, and sometimes more often, but this was the first time in almost as many years as I'd been away that I'd been back at the time of the state fair. Though my own days of rooster-crowing contests and 4-H projects and prize-winning bell peppers now seemed like a lifetime ago, from the second we entered the parking lot it had felt like just last week that I was here at the fair with my two older brothers, perusing the industrial building, prepping for the swine show, going to see everyone from the local country artists on the free stage to George Strait at the grandstand in full country garb from boots to hat. Every summer of my childhood had included the anticipation of those eleven days in August, and I had continued to frequent the fair, often with Isabel, throughout my high school years and right up to the summer before I left home.

Isabel still looked the quintessential cowgirl in her no-pocket Wrangler jeans and brown, round-toe, lace-up boots. There was a time when we were younger when we often looked like twins, side by side in our similar country-girl styles and ubiquitous cowboy boots, all of which we often traded back and forth. My country wardrobe had long since been discarded or donated, down to the last pair of boots I owned up until the day I took off for the East Coast. I was leaving that identity behind me, packing up for a shiny new one in the land of skyscrapers and glamour and busy streets—and, I had found, relentless pacing, ubiquitous traffic and pervasive pollution. Give and take.

Isabel had offered to lend me a pair of boots for the day. I had taken her up on the offer for old times' sake, pairing the pointed-toe, white-stitched, black leather style with a pair of cutoffs, a look I'd sported commonly during my teenage years. The outfit soon felt as familiar as the fair itself, even as I sensed the irrevocable distance of almost ten years in some intangible way. I was grateful for the sturdiness of the steel and leather that hugged my feet as we picked our way over the mud-formed tire tracks and stiff peaks of earth the rain earlier in the week had left on our route to the livestock area.

It was between the sheep and cattle barns that I saw him. He was dressed like a cowboy, which didn't really set him apart around here. The features and physique that made him look like Christian Bale in a hat, however, certainly did. My eyes barely had time to run from the black felt to the slate-gray boots he had on before gravitating magnetically to his eyes—which were looking at mine.

My lips parted, and instinctively I took a step toward him. There were twenty-five yards separating us, but I noticed nothing that was between us as my gaze zeroed in on him like a laser. It was a focus I didn't really even feel like I controlled; it was simply how I looked at people I wanted to fuck.

For a second he held my gaze, and I couldn't tell for sure if it reflected what was in mine before a wave of people intersected the distance between us, sweeping him from sight as Isabel asked what I was doing and nudged me along. I looked back as we approached the cattle barn, but none of the plethora of black cowboy hats in view sat atop the specimen of walking masculine sex appeal I had just glimpsed.

As we entered the cattle barn, my focus had already crystallized around finding him. Of course, the probability of such was low; though I felt quite content now to remain on the premises until my flight back East was scheduled to depart the day after tomorrow, the fair would close before then. Even in the several hours we had between then and now, we were unlikely to encounter him again among the hundreds of acres and tens of thousands of fair attendees surrounding us.

Such logic did nothing to stop the fixation on meeting him from rising up and locking into place inside me. Large fans blasted furiously from the corners of the animals' stalls as I turned my attention to the cows around us. The air was sticky with the notorious Midwestern August humidity, and Isabel fanned her top away from her chest as we walked out the other side of the cattle barn back into the searing afternoon sunlight. I blinked and scanned the swirling crowd, an activity my eyes rarely stopped for the next few hours as we perused the karaoke stage, took refuge in the air-conditioned 4-H exhibit building and stopped for ice cream on our way to the state historic display property.

All, alas, to no avail.

"I want to ride the sky glider," Isabel said as she polished off her ice-cream cone. "That'll take us over to the agriculture building, and then we'll be close to the midway when it gets dark."

Treetops moved slowly by and then below us as the ski-lift-like ride of colored roofs connected to benches with backs

inched along its suspension. Isabel hung her arm out the side of
our bright blue one, tilting her face up to the sun.

"I've always found this ride so relaxing," she said.

"Nothing like being suspended fifty feet in the air in a box
held up by a wire." I was about to comment further when I saw
a black cowboy hat beneath us to our left. That wasn't much of
a stretch, since there was a ratio of about one black cowboy hat
per four people at the fair, but I sensed the distinctiveness of this
particular figure and craned my neck to look past Isabel. A jolt
sizzled through me as I caught a glimpse of slate-gray boots.

I almost swore out loud, maddened by the re-spotting of him
at a time when there was nothing I could do to make contact with
him. I glanced at a passing tree, pondering for a split second the
effectiveness of dropping into it and climbing to the ground as my
cowboy, facing away from us, receded in the opposite direction.

"What are you doing?" Isabel asked, turning toward where I
looked as I practically climbed on top of her to keep sight of my
visual target. "You see somebody you want to fuck, don't you?"
she demanded as she looked back at me. "You have that primal
look you get when that's become your focus."

I ignored her, trying to discern where the cowboy might be
headed as our sky box crept along at the pace of a sloth swimming through honey. As we began to slope downward, a large
maple tree emerged between us and the ground, neatly eradi-
cating my view of him.

"Dammit," I swore as I sat back.

"Is it someone you know?" Isabel asked, looking in the direction of the tree.

"Not yet," I said as we approached the disembarkation
station. "And at this point I probably won't, since I'm not likely
to find him again in this crowd."

"Hard as I know you'll try to!" Isabel said cheerfully as we stepped off the ride. I glowered at her as she linked arms with me, turning us toward the agricultural building as she continued her uninvited monologue. "Well, if you're looking to get laid— which I'm sure you are because I've never known you not to be—I'm sure you'll find someone amongst the eighty thousand people here who does it for you. It's like the famous fair food," she added as she glanced at the jam-packed food concourse. "Just about anything you've got a taste for, you can find here."

I didn't respond. Admittedly, Isabel was right; there probably was someone satisfactory I could find for the purpose. But having seen the Christian Bale look-alike, it would be like settling for fast food (or deep-fried cheesecake) after knowing filet mignon was in the vicinity.

"We'll see." My tone indicated the closing of the conversation.

"Oh, hey look, it's Lisa," Isabel said, raising her arm and calling out. I turned to see Lisa with two other of our high school friends smiling as they headed toward us. It had been a couple years since I'd seen any of them, and we exchanged warm greetings as the five of us congregated under the cover of a sycamore tree.

Dusk was beginning to hover, and the multitude of nighttime lights started to blink on all around the nearby midway. Although lighting up randomly, the myriad small, large, clear and colored bulbs seemed like a cued light show as they seized attention and bounced it from one attraction to another until the entire area was a gleaming display of sparkling lights.

I checked out of the conversation for a moment to observe the natural light in the form of the sunset lounging casually along the horizon. Its effortless peacefulness was contagious, and I took a deep breath and felt my body relax a notch as I turned back to Isabel and company.

And there he was. Right on the other side of the path, standing with his friends at the edge of the midway as they engaged in animated conversation. He wasn't looking at me this time, but as I stared, he turned his head. He did a double take as he caught my eye.

I held his gaze, throwing an "I'll catch up with you guys later" over my shoulder as I started across the asphalt. I heard the smile in Isabel's voice behind me as she filled our friends in on what I was undoubtedly doing. I didn't turn around, but I could sense the quartet grinning in support at my back as my cowboy maintained eye contact with me while I crossed the expanse between us. As I approached he took a few steps away from his friends to meet me at the edge of the path.

"Hi." I held out my hand. "I'm June."

"Travis," he said, shaking it. Sparks shot from where our skin touched to every extremity in my body as he seemed in no hurry to let go. He looked me up and down. "Are you from around here?"

"Visiting," I said. "I live in New York."

He nodded, glancing down at my boots. "I thought so." I raised my eyebrows, and he grinned a little. "You're dressed the part, but I get a city-girl vibe from you somehow. I just guessed you weren't local."

I smiled, finding I had to work slightly to keep the wistfulness from showing in it. Years ago I would have been thrilled by such a comment. I wasn't sure now how it struck me that I seemed so obviously out of place here.

"Does that mean you are?" I asked.

He nodded and named a small town in the southern part of the state, a couple of hours away from my own hometown and the fairgrounds themselves.

"So, June." His eyes shifted to the midway. "Can I interest

you in a ferris wheel ride?"

I hid a smile. Travis was looking to break the ice. He didn't understand yet that there was no ice with me—it was long melted, the water cool and inviting and just waiting for an occupant.

I leaned toward him almost imperceptibly. "Actually, the tilt-a-whirl's a little more my speed," I said as I held his gaze.

There was the slightest of pauses before he gave an agreeable nod, and his countenance was impassive as he gestured toward the midway. The uncertainty of this reception seemed to fuel the desire in me, and arousal coiled in my stomach as I fell into step beside him, my borrowed black boots striking the pavement rhythmically.

We entered the crowded midway, where excited screams overlapped the whistles and jingles of various games and attractions and hundreds of multilevel voices. Gears and levers cranked around us as we approached the tilt-a-whirl, and we waited in the short line for the current ride to come to an end. Travis pulled a folded stack of tickets from his pocket as he approached the conductor, and our matching boot thumps rattled the metal as we ascended the steps and walked around to a car. Travis stepped back to let me in, flashing me a smile as I slid past him and dropped onto the bench. I watched out of the corner of my eye as he settled in beside me.

"I hope this ride's okay with you," it occurred to me to say.

Travis's grin made me catch my breath, and suddenly there was no longer a question that we both knew what we were doing. "It's fine with me. I just wanted to offer something slow to start with, not knowing what you liked."

The ride began to move, crawling slowly for the first few seconds. "Yeah, I'm more of a wild ride girl myself," I said lightly as I rested my hands on the silver safety bar.

The momentum built, intermittent screams beginning around us as the ride grew to full swing. I smiled as gravity and inertia yanked us forward and backward, ramming us into each other as our car spun wildly at unpredictable intervals. I let out an involuntary shriek as we whipped into an uncontrolled spin that pressed me against Travis's hard body. He grinned at me, and the characteristic adrenaline the ride had elicited rushed straight to my pussy.

My hand landed on Travis's thigh a few moments later as the ride jammed us together again, and I turned my head to maneuver my mouth near his ear. "Do you come to the fair a lot?" I almost had to shout over the noise of the wind, the ride, and the screams of our fellow riders.

He nodded. "My parents own a business that sells farm machinery and livestock equipment. They rent a space in the machinery lot for display, and I help them staff it. So I spend a lot of time here."

Our car jolted, and conversation was suspended as we flew into a vortex-like spiral. I squealed, breathless with laugher by the time the car pitched the opposite direction and held us in a vigorous swing from side to side. I looked back at him.

"I see," I said in response to his last comment. I saw the conductor reach for the lever that would bring the ride to its eventual end, and I moved my mouth close to Travis's ear again. "So, Travis," I said imitating his earlier inflection. I paused, feeling the ride begin to slow down. "If you find yourself so inclined to show me, I'd love to take a look at your equipment." I set my hand on his thigh again, higher up this time, and bit my lip as I resisted the urge to slide it up to his crotch and grasp the bulge I was almost sure would be there.

Travis's jaw clenched, and I saw him reach for my wrist. My breath caught when he touched it, sliding my hand up himself to position it on the hard cock beneath his jeans. My pussy spilled over as our car rose and dipped on the platform, the speed decreasing until we came to a stop.

I shook myself as Travis lifted the safety bar, and we both stood up. We didn't exchange a word as I followed him off the ride and back down the steps. As our boots hit the grass, he took my hand and led me to the edge of the midway, out of the plethora of blinking lights into the quieter fairgrounds, past buildings still lit up but lacking the bustle they had claimed during the daylight hours.

He walked me into the darkened machinery area, the motionless collection of gleaming metal behemoths surrounded by silence in the sparse glow of the few thirty-five-foot lights surrounding the lot. We walked past cutters and plows and grain augers to a cluster of livestock trailers arranged on the grass.

The smaller-sized fully enclosed livestock trailer stood mostly in shadow, one corner of the silver metal gleaming with the reflection of a distant light. Travis lowered the door and turned to me. Before I could step forward, he pushed into me and wrapped his arms around my waist as his tongue slid against mine with a promise that left me breathless.

He broke away and gestured in invitation, and I stepped up into the trailer, the echo of boot on metal sounding loud in the hot stillness. Travis climbed in behind me and closed the door. Then he reached for me in the darkness, his mouth on mine as I lowered myself to the floor, pulling him on top of me. He removed his hat and set it off to the side.

Despite the temperature, the metal against my back was cool, spiking the heat between us with a contrast like sweet and savory together. Travis worked the buttons of the sleeveless blouse I wore, and I arched my back as he pulled my bra off and lowered his mouth to a nipple. I sighed as he reached to pull open my cutoffs.

Backing up, Travis pulled my shorts and panties off, and I gasped as he dove without warning between my legs, his mouth warm on my pussy before I could catch my breath. His tongue was insistent, strong, enthusiastic without being the least bit impatient, and I moaned as it was instantly obvious that Travis was a man who loved to eat pussy. A squeal as involuntary as the one on the tilt-a-whirl escaped me as I squirmed, and my nerve endings started to tingle with the orgasm I knew was imminent. Travis rested a hand on my belly, and I took a breath, feeling suspended for a moment before my scream shattered the air as he made me come with his tongue, my body thrashing against the metal beneath me as I bucked and wailed and clutched at his hair, my voice echoing off the walls of our tiny aluminum chamber.

Travis rose up to his knees, ripping open his fly as I panted beneath him. I whimpered at the sight of the rock-hard cock that sprang from his jeans, running my hands over the sheen of sweat that covered my body as I arched my back. He pulled a condom from his pocket, and I smiled.

He noticed. "I like to keep one on me, just in case." His smile was a bit sheepish as he shrugged.

"Seems to be paying off tonight." My voice was still breathless. Travis was still for a moment, and so that he didn't get the wrong idea—that I felt slighted by the thought of his doing this on a regular basis, that I was offended by the idea of his being with other women—I told him, truthfully: "I do the same thing."

He grinned back then, and the shared understanding of what we both wanted brought us ironically closer right then, the purity of our connection strengthened in the understood congruence of our intention. I took the package from him and ripped it open, and his breath hitched as I slid the rubber down his hard cock. The second I was done he pushed me back, barely giving me time to whisper "Fuck me" before he plunged into my body and my hips rose to meet him, his hand cushioning the back of my head against the hard, cool floor.

I screamed again as Travis pounded me, the echo of metal reverberating around us. Through the slots in the side of the trailer I could see the sky glider inching along in the distance, and I smiled at the forgotten frustration of hours before when I'd caught sight of him from up in the air.

Travis ran his other hand through my hair, and I turned my head to catch his thumb lightly between my teeth, running my tongue up his salty skin as his pace increased and he came inside me, grasping my hair as I felt his muffled groan against my shoulder. I lay beneath him, reveling in the deep relaxation of my body as he kissed my neck gently and lifted himself from me.

After we were dressed, Travis opened the door, and I jumped to the grass and turned back while he closed it.

"Livestock trailer," he said with a grin at me as he secured the door, nodding at the trailer.

But I knew what it was. I smiled in the darkness. I didn't tell him I was from here, that I had grown up on a farm thirty miles from the spot where we stood. Really there was nothing in the rows of giant equipment surrounding us that I couldn't identify. When my brothers and I were kids we were privy to perpetual reminders not to play on or near the machinery—an understandable reprimand given the danger farm equipment could pose under the guise of its deceivingly innocuous appearance.

We walked back out to the fairgrounds, toward the midway where we stopped just before the whirlwind of lights and sounds.

Travis turned to me. "Have a safe trip home, city girl," he said, tilting his hat up as he bent to kiss me.

I smiled and kissed him back, bypassing for the last time the chance to correct him. He probably didn't encounter too many "city girls" at the fair, and I'd let him keep the fantasy—even as I knew, deep down, that I wasn't one either. We set off in different directions, and I pulled my phone out to text Isabel. When I looked over my shoulder, he did too, and he grinned and waved. I waved back, both of us bidding good-bye to the "city girl" who was as much a figment of my imagination as she was of his.

SUBWAY
SUBTERFUGE

May Deva

The first day I saw him, he was standing on the subway platform, a few feet to the left and ahead of me slightly. There was something about his neck just where it met his collar; I wanted to know what that muscle felt like between my teeth, under my tongue. I wiggled through the crowd, trying to get a closer look. The train screamed to a halt, throwing open the doors before I could get my eye-candy fix. I rushed into the same car, but lost him in the shuffle. As I was leaving the car at my stop, I caught a glimpse of smoldering eyes and a half-hidden face as I scanned the car one more time. Smiling, I filed it under "Interesting" and moved into my day.

He had faded from my thoughts when he reappeared a week later. He stood in exactly the same spot, no suit this time, But a worn leather jacket and, heaven help me, dark indigo denim. I jostled to get closer, without much luck. He turned his head as the train groaned to a stop in front of us and our eyes met. Pinned by his dark gaze, I watched his lips curve slightly and his face register my interest. Caught, I flushed and looked away but was swept into the car by the people around me. I tried not to look for him, but I have always been too curious for my own good. No sign of him. *Damn.* I sighed, steeled myself for my workday and tried not to think of eyes that held dark secrets and promised wonderful things. As I stepped out of the car, something brushed my hip. I looked down to see a hand, and the cuff of a worn leather jacket, disappear behind me into the crowd. On the platform, I turned to look, but there was no sign of him.

Later that day, on my way to lunch, I put my hand into my coat pocket, searching for a lipstick. What I found was far more valuable. A small white card with elegant masculine script:

I see you, too. Want to play?— M.

I swear I could smell leather.

The next morning, I got to the station earlier than normal. I had fussed with my clothes and hair—I wore a swingy skirt, scoop-neck blouse and loose chignon. Utterly ridiculous to be exerting this kind of effort over a stranger, but it was nice to have someone actually notice me. In a big city, that was rare. I was horribly disappointed though, when he was nowhere to be seen. The rest of the day dragged by, and quitting time was a relief indeed. Waiting on the platform, I wondered if I might see my mystery guy tomorrow morning, wondered idly what I might wear, if it might rain.

Sun-warmed leather filled my nostrils, alerting me to his presence long before I saw him. He was behind me, I was sure of it, sure I could feel his breath wafting across my bare neck. My pulse picked up. I heard the train rumbling toward the station and decided to make sure. I turned quickly and found myself inches from a sexy smirk, those eyes boring into mine. His eyes held mine for a moment, dropped to my lips, down to my breasts then back up. Smirk widened to grin as I tried to hold his gaze and failed. People began to move around us, propelling us into the waiting car as well.

His fingers shot lightning up my arm as he circled my wrist, leading me toward the back of the car. He turned to face me at the end of the aisle. This time, I didn't drop my eyes, didn't try to hide the interest and arousal that was evident in them. Slowly, he moved his hand from my wrist, tracing up my arm to my shoulder and turning me to face the front of the car.

Puzzled, I surveyed the crowded car, standing room only at this point in the day. Everyone looked either tired or preoccupied. His hand slid back down my arm, lingering inside my wrist, then traveling back up my arm again. The train lurched into motion as I grabbed the rail with my free hand. Fingers lightly traced the edge of my blouse across the back of my neck, bringing my nipples to swift attention, then continuing up the side of my neck and behind my ear, following my hairline and moving back down again. The feel of his fingers lingered on my skin after they moved on. Both hands slid down my arms slowly, then settled at my waist. He pulled me backward into him, moving one hand across my stomach to keep me there, the other hand slipping slowly up my side. I held my breath as fingertips brushed up the side of my breast, inscribed tiny whorls over and over again.

The train slid to a stop, the motion pressing a nicely firm cock against my ass. I grinned, now sure that I wasn't the only one getting all hot and bothered. As the car began to move again, I shifted my hips subtly to press a little harder against him, using the swaying rhythm for extra oomph. I felt one twitch of his cock, then another. I was feeling pretty smug when I felt lips against the nape of my neck and I stilled. He gave a swirl of his tongue at the base and I moaned out loud. A puff of breath against my skin let me know that he was amused, which prompted me to resume my subtle lap dance. His hand dropped to my hip, pulling me even tighter against him, making me more aware of each movement while his lips continued to explore the back of my neck. My heart was tripping; I was getting wetter by the minute.

There was another stop and exchange of passengers, the last before my own. I felt him flex his knees slightly, then his fingers on my bare thigh underneath my skirt. He trailed his nails up the back of my leg, gave another chuckle when I wriggled against him with pleasure. I turned my head, trying not to moan again, and he captured my earlobe between his teeth—sucking and biting at the same time. I was coming undone, quickly. I slid my hand behind me, flexing my fingers over his jean-clad cock, tracing its shape and smirking when he groaned softly in my ear. Delicious.

All too soon I felt the train slow and knew my stop was near. Now what? I certainly couldn't invite a stranger to my apartment. Tipping my head back, I reached up to pull his lips to mine. His heat poured between my lips, left me breathless yet again and wanting more. As the doors slid open, I broke away regretfully.

"Wait. What's your name?"

His voice was as deep as his eyes, mellifluous and sexy as hell. A smile lit his face as he waited for my answer.

I grinned and tipped a wink as I stepped through the doors. "I'll tell you tomorrow."

PERFORMANCE ART

Cynthia Hamilton

The single droplet trailed its lazy way down the curve of the model's bare, goosefleshed ass. It shone amber like bottled sunset, too thin to be honey, but too viscous to be wine. *Nectar,* Julie thought, and suddenly she could taste its burst of sweetness and imagine the texture of the cool, aroused skin it traveled. The golden droplet was so large and clear on the high resolution screen, such a contrast to the gray scale of the woman's skin, that Julie found her breath catching in her throat, caught up in the suspense of waiting for the quivering drop to fall. A small pond on the museum's floor below the projection screen rippled outward from its center in perfect synchrony, accompanied by a delicate *plink* of sound.

Julie smiled. The illusion was seamless, and she felt her own inner moisture stirring in response. Instead of seeing the thin line the liquid was leaving behind, she imagined the broader swath that would be evidence of her tongue's passing. What would it feel like to be so wet; to be so aware of the fall of every individual drop?

After an afternoon of wandering through explicit art installations, she was dangerously close, she thought, to finding out.

It was a rainy European day, the sort that the guidebooks had warned her about, but that she hadn't really taken seriously enough when she'd made the impulsive decision to stay an extra few days past the end of the conference.

Outside, the afternoon was as gray as the model's black-and-white ass, though not nearly as clearly focused or as inviting. Few other tourists had chosen refuge in the gallery, perhaps because of its theme. A handful or two milled about, a room or so ahead, and another scattered few wandered at her pace. None of them seemed to be responding to the exhibits as she was.

On the screen, another amber droplet had started its slow, inevitable glide. She longed for it, as if some part of her thought that catching it on her tongue might fill her with the brilliant heat that the day—the whole trip, so far—had lacked. The Lucite-protected plaque on the wall, mounted nearby but out of the way, would contain a description of the medium. She browsed her way toward it. She had to know what kind of liquid trailed single file down the woman's lush cheek.

And the plaque might have held such information. But not in English.

Plink.

Julie frowned, tugging at faint, distant strands of high-school French. The restless simmer of arousal made it hard to think.

"Excuse me." A voice came from behind her ear—smooth, male—along with the faintest touch to her shoulder. "*Français?*"

Julie inhaled a shallow breath. *Plink:* another drop of nectar. She shivered.

"No, sorry," she answered quietly, turning. He was just a little taller than she was, slender, with black hair that had dried in short, unruly curls from the rain. She associated the combination of blue eyes and dark hair with Europeans, but his voice was a welcome piece of home.

Her cheeks burned. She lifted her cool hands to them. But he only smiled. He wore layers: open jacket over a dark sweater, and a collared blue shirt and a black T-shirt underneath.

"American?" he asked. He was in his midthirties. Professional. Confident. A lawyer, or a writer, maybe. She glanced down at his hands when she nodded. No ring.

"San Diego," she answered, and her stomach fluttered. She wasn't sure if she hoped he'd turn out to live near, or far.

"Portland," he said. Then, "David."

"Ju— *Je m'appelle* Sarah," Julie answered. Why had she done that? He was so close she could smell his expensive cologne, and she could barely think over the swell of anticipation that filled her chest and buzzed in her ears, waiting for the next drip of golden nectar. She floundered a moment, caught in his eyes, then smiled sheepishly. She blurted out the next thing that occurred to her, to cover her stumbled deception: "That's the only French I know."

He laughed politely. "You know more than I do, then. But I love to listen to it. It's a beautiful tongue."

Tongues... She wasn't imagining her tongue gliding up that model's flesh anymore; she was imagining his tongue, on her.

When she turned away to move on, she could almost feel her wetness pooling. Overflowing.

The next exhibit was a pair of screens. The top display, above Julie's eye level, featured a pair of feminine hands cuffed to either end of a Lucite spreader bar. At ground level, a pair of masculine feet were cuffed to another bar. Both sets of extremities moved in unison, as if they belonged to a single invisible person—a person being thoroughly, roughly, unendingly taken from behind. This piece, like the ones before it, had a soundtrack: a looped recording of elevated breaths over the rhythmic clink of chain. Watching the straining, clenched hands made the sound of the breathing seem more feminine. Looking at the feet turned the perception of it more masculine.

Closing her eyes entirely, Julie perceived it as her own.

"Wow," David murmured beside her. "That's…" He swallowed. "Hot."

Julie's cheeks burned. "Yeah," she whispered. Her lips felt dry and reluctant to move. She swept them with her tongue. "I'm glad I'm not the only one this place is…you know. Getting to."

His hand brushed hers, radiating warmth. It couldn't have been an accident, no matter how hard her racing mind tried to convince her that it had to be. She spread her fingers, an invitation, and his returned to hers. They interlaced, and the touch tingled all the way through her and took her breath away. It was a long few minutes before she realized she was squeezing his hand in time with the thrusts of the invisible bodies before her.

He realized it, too. She started to pull away, feeling as though she should feel ashamed, but he gripped her hand reassuringly and let out a weighted sigh. It was low and uneven, almost but not quite a moan, and it was quite possibly the most sensual sound she'd ever heard. Suddenly she wanted more than anything to coax that sound out of him again; to know she'd been the cause of it.

They moved on, hand in hand. Occasionally he stroked the heel of her palm with his thumb. It made her shiver.

A close hallway was next, lined on both sides with hints that anonymous figures rested nearly submerged in the plaster. The slight swells of breasts and thighs, chests and cocks, shoulder blades and rumps presented themselves for the fondling and amusement of all who passed. It was slightly discomforting, perhaps because Julie pictured herself as one of them, subject to random gropes, intimate yet thoughtless. There wasn't room for two to walk side by side, so David drew her hand behind her and let her walk ahead. Her boots were loud in the narrow corridor, and she said, "Excuse me" without thinking when her elbow bumped a plaster breast. She waited for David's laugh, but it didn't come. Instead he stopped, turned her toward the wall, and splayed her hand over one cool, subtle swell, squeezing the faux breast through her palm. Then, boldly, he shifted her willing hand to the curve of her own bosom and did the same.

Her heart caught in her throat. Somewhere far away a droplet of nectar fell, making an illusory ripple in an artificial pond. She could feel it.

The corridor ended in relative darkness, making a sharp left-hand turn. She heard the next piece before she saw it: soft wet sounds. An alcove was filled with flickering golden light to evoke the flame of candles, illuminating a mattress on the floor with punched-up pillows and rumpled white sheets.

Kissing. She was listening to slow, intensely intimate kissing. Beside her, David shivered and she moved closer, until their hips touched. It was wrong, what her senses were sharing with her. A couple was making out on that bed, she was sure of it; their invisibility was the illusion, not the lush sounds of lips meeting and parting.

Julie didn't at first realize that her chin was being lifted, that she was tilting her head, that she was sighing into David's breath. She wasn't aware of the moment his lips touched hers, only that the kiss was perfectly right. Now the sound fit. That little sigh of his—or was it hers? Mouthing at his lower lip. The sultry sounds of lips meeting, exploring, parting only to meet again.

Thinking back later, she would be fairly sure that she was the one to cross the velvet rope, to pull him down on top of her on the mussed sheets, locking him against her with a leg hooked around the back of his thigh.

But only fairly sure.

The mattress was Jell-O-soft and thin, like a day-old marshmallow left out in the heat. It had looked fluffy, but it shrank instantly to the floor under the slightest pressure. Julie didn't care, and neither did David. Without a thought to the other patrons, he soon had her shirt unbuttoned down to her waist, and pushed it off her shoulders. He stroked her back while his lips found hers again. They kissed, kissed some more, kissed to match the sounds in the soundtrack, kissed to defy them, but always their mouths touched, teased, claimed.

She thought nothing of the ticklish slide of her bra strap down her arm, nothing of the patrons wandering by with their tired expressions, glancing in at their flickering, mattress-clad world for a moment, getting bored and moving on. This wasn't for them. It was for her.

David's hands were spidery and nimble, perfect hands. They squeezed her breasts, weighing them in his palms, closing his fingers. At her encouragement, he pressed almost tightly enough to bruise. She moaned softly, a sound that caught the attention of a few of the browsers. She almost stopped, but he leaned in and caught her ear with his teeth. "Don't worry about them. It's only us," he murmured against her skin. He bit down, and she shuddered. Yes. She could ignore them. For him, for this chance with him, she could do that. For that warm rush of sensation and breath, the weight of him against her, she would have done anything he asked.

She snuck all his mismatched layers out of his waistband, finally finding warm chest to slide her hands against. The kissing sound resumed and they met it hotly, tongues playing and teasing. Her hips shifted from side to side in anticipation of having something between her thighs to ride, and she hurried his damned layers up past his chest. He stopped her, looked pointedly at her clothing—at the bra dangling off her shoulders, dark purple seeming black in the flickering gold of fake candlelight. The meaningful gaze moved downward, toward her waist. *If his clothes come off, mine come off? Okay. Small price to pay.*

She nodded her assent and reached for his gathered hems again. He sat up, and in true guy fashion, he grabbed the back collar and pulled the shirts over the top of his head as one. Even thinner without the insulating layers, he was almost delicate. *Lovely,* Julie thought. *And hopefully delicious.* She rose and leaned forward to find out.

His nipple was pert and hard, not one of those male nipples that hides down flat. As her tongue grazed and circled it, his hands tightened at her back and a gasp escaped his throat. *Oh, good. I like men who like this,* she thought, and surrendered her full attention to the little nub. Now the kissing noises had their match again—her lips surrounding his nipple, pulling at it, pressing in and suckling at it with teasing swirls of her tongue. Oh, it was good. Judging by the arch of his back and the squirm of his hips, he seemed to deeply appreciate the noisy kisses. She trailed a hand down his writhing side and over the front of his hip, finding the object of her search in the opened fly of his jeans: Hard and smooth, with a wetness of its own. Wet like the kisses she was planting on his nipples. Wet as if she'd already glided messy kisses down his cock.

Julie shuddered again, the curl of her hand tightening around his length. His fingers touched up under her chin, lifting her eyes. His were almost colorless in the uneven light, amused but also full of hunger. She shifted her hips. Her panties, soaked, clung to her.

"It's about desire," one patron said to another, a rare and unexpected voice in English behind her. "See how they're touching each other and disheveled, but not completely undressed? See how they're looking at each other, over those sounds? It's like we're hearing them think about their desire."

David grinned at Julie, and she grinned back. Still holding her chin, he leaned in to claim her lips in another dizzying kiss, matching the heated kisses filtering through the speakers. When her bra came off, Julie made sure to crumple it into an artful ball with her blouse. The air was cool on her nipples, and she felt her lower abdomen tighten. But a moment later his bare chest was against hers, warming her. The English tourists were still watching from the safety of the velvet ropes, accepting her anonymous encounter—her wanton, spontaneous, crazy display of random lust—because they believed it to be scripted for their entertainment.

David's fingers tightened on her chin. "Not for them," he breathed at her lips between hard, humid kisses. "For us."

Julie nodded shallowly. Her hand had stilled on him, and now she stirred it into motion again, fishing his cock fully out of his jeans and stroking his slickness along his shaft. He groaned into her mouth, surged in her fist. He was a little thicker than she was used to, she thought, and perhaps a little longer. She blazed with the need to know how he would feel inside her.

He slid a hand up under her skirt and into her tights, faltering with a sharp intake of breath when he reached her slippery labia. The feel of his bare fingers sent a hard tingle through her core. If he'd had any doubt as to the extent of her arousal, he didn't any more. "Smooth," he told her lips between kisses. One finger squirmed its way to the snugness of her entrance.

"Soaked," she answered. The single word came out more apologetically than she'd meant it to.

"I like soaked," he murmured, shifting his wrist to spear his fingers in deeply and prove his point. They spread her, curving perfectly to the shape of her body, but didn't fill her quite full enough. She rocked on his hand. "Mmm. And needy. I like needy, too."

She was sure she was blushing, but she didn't care. She rode his fingers, pushing them harder against all the right places inside her. Then they were gone, and wet fingers were tugging down her tights. She leaned back on the thin mattress and lifted her rear. Her skirt pooled around her waist, obscuring her sex from the patrons but not from him. He waited, tights around her ankles, while she kicked off her boots, then pulled the ribbed cotton off her feet with her thick walking socks still attached to them. There was a moment of shyness, of feeling exposed and aware of the gathering crowd, and then he was crawling back up her body with his jeans around his thighs, the wet sounds of kissing still charging the air around her, and she forgot about everything else.

Strong fingers spread her legs, glided lightly up her slippery labia, and parted them. Then his lips were around her clit, suckling to give new depth to the intimate sounds that surrounded them. Deep, intense, just the way he'd kissed her mouth, surrounding her folds with warmth and delving between them to drink in more of her nectar.

Her climax took her by surprise, but it didn't surprise him. He held her thighs, pinned down and open, caressing her sensitive places with the flat of his tongue long after her tremors would have otherwise ceased. Only when she reached down to his hair did he rise, crawling up her body and settling the smooth heat of his penis against her drenched skin. His hips rolled once, rubbing him through her wetness, and she was rewarded with another of his perfect, hungry moans. His kisses tasted sweet and forbidden, wetting her lips with her own arousal.

She pressed herself to the firmness of his shaft, grinding her hips to push her clit against his pelvic bone. He took her chin again, forcing her gaze to his in the flickering light. "Yes?" he asked. His cock pulsed against her entrance, poised and waiting.

Disjointed words flooded through her mind. *On the pill* was too long for her lips to be away from his. *Tested. Clean. Consenting.* All true, but only fragments of what she wanted to convey. She shifted her hips, and he moaned again. She could feel his arms trembling with the effort of holding his body above hers. She could hear the murmurs of the onlookers under the wet sounds, so like the ones his mouth had made on her cunt. And then, on their own, her lips formed the word that meant all of those yeses and also *Now*.

"*Please.*"

He drove into her without a moment's pause, filling her with all the fullness and length she'd hoped for. She arched up against him, legs rising, feet hooking on the backs of his thighs and finding denim there. She squeezed his cock inside her, and a strangled groan accompanied his next thrust. His lips crushed down onto hers and he fucked her with a steady pace—firm and measured, accompanied by the low claps of bodies joining and the slick, lewd liquid noise that was evidence of her overflowing desire.

"Sarah..." he gasped at her lips.

It took her a moment—a quick moment, measured in three thrusts—to remember.

"Yes." Breathy and low, her answer was encouragement as much as confirmation.

"Sarah, I'm close."

The words were low, like a growl, and they sent a thrill through her. She tightened her thighs around his, digging her heels in, and felt her sex constrict around his cock. One pulse, then another, and suddenly she couldn't breathe. It welled up in her, each pulse rippling outward like the droplets in the pond, filling her with sensation until she couldn't help but brim over.

He buried a strangled cry in the curve of her neck, clutching her tightly to him and pounding her into the thin mattress. Her arms around him, she leaned up and trailed kisses along his bare shoulder, matching the sounds of insatiable passion that still surrounded them. He groaned, filling her with molten heat just when she thought she would burst, pulling her over the edge with him.

He relaxed on her gradually. They rode out the climax with slow, dreamy shifts of their hips. Afterward, when the last of his deep pulses had triggered the last of hers, he grazed her jaw with his teeth. He seemed in no hurry to move, and that was good. Julie's body was all tingle and no substance, finally rid of the pressure that had been building in her all day. She didn't think she could have gotten up if she had to. Even if the artist and the museum staff were to suddenly arrive with the police, she thought, she would only be able to move far enough to invite them to join in.

"It's about afterglow," one patron was telling another. Her accent, Scottish and gentle, floated lyrically above the quieter murmurs. "See how they're laying there entwined, with the glow of a fireplace, and the clothes and bedding scattered around them, and the sound of slow, aftermath kissing."

"You don't know that," Julie heard another woman answer her. "It's art. It's what we make of it."

David heard them, too. His arms tightened around her in a warm squeeze, and he winked one pale blue eye at her.

It was indeed.

LET SLEEPING DOGS COME

Chrissie Bentley

W hat's the most common lie that a guy tells his girlfriend?"
Sharon's eyes were glittering with delight.

Mary shook her head. "I don't know."

"'I promise I won't come in your mouth.' And what's the most common lie a girl tells him?"

"I don't know."

"'Good.'"

Mary smiled briefly and then frowned. "I don't get it."

"Oh. come on. 'I won't come in your mouth'—'Good.' The two biggest lies."

I sank down in my seat. Someone once told Sharon she was South Philly's answer to the singer Amy Winehouse, and I'm not sure that they meant it nicely. It's the accent, I think, an unholy cross between fingernails on a chalkboard, and a fax machine that smokes too much. But I love her to bits, and I love to see her in full flight as well. She's hours of fun, she laughs like a gurgling drain, and if you don't understand her sense of humor, she might as well be speaking Swahili. Which, judging from the look on Mary's face, is what she's doing right now.

"Okay, let me spell it out for you." Slowly, patiently, and a lot more facetiously than could ever have been necessary, Sharon explained her not-so-funny joke, then turned to me in triumph. "Chrissie gets it, don't you Chrissie?"

I nodded.

"Every time," Sharon concluded, then threw her head back in a violent laugh.

Mary looked at me curiously. "Really? And you like it?"

I paused. "What was that line from *Sex and the City*? 'Well, it's not a trip to Baskin-Robbins, but....'"

"I had a guy who worked at Baskin-Robbins once. He was hot." Sharon hooted again at her (admittedly labored) oxymoron, but Mary at last was on solid ground. "And I had a pizza delivery guy, only he arrived too quickly. I mean 'came.' He came too quickly." I laughed and was about to add my own pun to the party when a shadow fell across us. "And if you ladies have finished with your undoubtedly scintillating conversation, the seminar is about to resume."

We gathered our purses, rose and followed Mr. Albertson out of the cafeteria. Great—the three of us had tugged so many corporate strings in order to wrangle our places at the book fair...the biggest in the country, held midsummer in New York...and our boss caught us laughing on the very first day. Good job he didn't see Sharon last night.

She had, from what she told us this morning, made quite the night of it. The book fair's not just for publishers, after all. There are authors here as well, and some of them...well, like the guy from Baskin-Robbins, they're hot. Or at least famous. So, when Sharon walked into the hotel bar, and spotted—oh, I'd better not say his name; suffice to say that he's exotic, balding and recently separated—she just had to leaf through his pages. And they both told each other lies. Apparently.

Me, I went to bed with a good book, and I expected to be doing the same thing tonight. Star-fucking's fine when you're in your early twenties, but it loses its luster after a while, especially when (as is so often the case) the star turns out to be a dick. A dick with a dick, granted. But a dick all the same.

We made our way into the auditorium and found our seats. The guest speaker—yes, it was Sharon's friend from last night, as her pointy elbows kept excitedly reminding me—was already at the podium, but while he registered our late arrival, he gave no sign of recognizing its loudest component. I wondered whether he might even be regretting having succumbed to her admittedly buxom charms. Sharon might be a dynamite editor, but she's scarcely the smoothest dildo in the drawer. In fact, she can be rather prickly.

I fixed my eyes on the speaker, doing my best to ignore Sharon's whispers and giggles, and when the guy seated in front of me turned around to try and stare her into silence, I offered him my sweetest sympathetic smile. Quite frankly, I don't think it's possible to shut Sharon up...even with her mouth full, she's probably drumming out Morse code with her fingernails. I'd hate to be within earshot when she orgasms.

Damn, but this guy was boring. I swore if he namedropped one more of his bloody awful books—"and as I wrote in blah blah blah..."—I couldn't help myself. "Please tell me," I hissed to Sharon, "that he wasn't this dull last night?"

She snorted. "Well, he is a bit full of himself," she half whispered. "Even fuller than I was, in fact." Again her laughter drowned out the speaker, and again the guy in front of us turned with an irritated look on his face. "Must be his agent," Sharon hissed, just loud enough for the man to hear. "Nobody else could care that much. Fucking old windbag."

I felt myself redden, out of sympathy as much as shock, watched as the man turned away from us, and I fought to straighten my face. The worst thing was, he was rather cute...the guy in front us, that is, not the author, who was now droning on about some existentialist dilemma that he dramatically resolved on page 474 of blah blah blah blah....

"You can wake up now, he's finished." I opened my eyes. Oh, my god, Mr. Albertson...no: it was the agent. Beside me, I could hear Sharon chattering away to whomever would listen, poor Mary probably, while around us, the rest of the audience was leaving.

I thought of trying to bluff my way out, but I knew it wouldn't work. "Did I miss much?"

"No. Nothing at all." He cast a nervous glance at Sharon and looked relieved when he realized she was oblivious to his presence. "I was wondering...it's my first time alone in New York. Would you be free for dinner this evening?"

"I'm not a writer, you know." After all, why else would a literary agent be asking me out?

"And I'm not his representative," he said pointedly, with another glance at Sharon. He fished around in his jacket pocket and pulled out a card. "Robin Mitchell—publisher." "Hey, you do..." I rattled off half a dozen book titles, a series that I'd been collecting for a few years, on the history of American pinup art.

He nodded. "And you are?"

I gave him my card. "Senior editor, eh? See, we have something in common already. I'll meet you in your hotel lobby at seven, yes?"

"Okay." I told him where I was staying, then sighed with relief as he stood and walked away, just as Sharon turned her attention back to me. "What was that all about?"

"He's a psychiatrist," I lied smilingly. "We were comparing notes on how to quiet unruly patients."

"Fucking nerve," she shrugged. "I'll tell you who needs a psychiatrist. That smug shit who just spent the last ninety minutes boring us to death talking about his books. I tell you, if he could fuck like he can talk, I'd still have him chained to the bed right now."

"Instead?" I ventured.

"Instead, I gave him a hand job in the lift, then went back to the bar and picked up the bellhop." She smiled apologetically. "Yeah, well it sounded a lot more glamorous the other way 'round, didn't it?"

Robin—funny, I've never known a male Robin before, apart from Robin Hood, but apparently it's common where he grew up—was there at seven on the dot. "I would have brought you flowers," he said as I appeared in the lobby. "But I didn't think you'd want to carry them around with you all evening."

I smiled. Actually, I'd rather he'd brought me a selection from his backlist—his company's books aren't cheap. "No worries. So where are we going?"

"To be honest, I wasn't sure, so I made reservations at my hotel restaurant. Which just happens to be your hotel restaurant as well. Small world, isn't it?"

"Very." Damn, I was rather hoping we'd be off somewhere else. The last person I wanted to see tonight was Sharon, but there wasn't much chance of avoiding her now. She'd already told me she was eating in this evening, in the hope of getting eaten out later.

Clearly, however, I'd underestimated my escort. Yes, we were in the hotel restaurant. But who knew that they had semiprivate rooms, just two or three tables, well screened from other diners, and insulated, too, from the noise of the lobby and the muzak in the elevators? "You can even hire violinists to sere-nade you while you eat," said Robin. "But I thought that might be pushing it a bit."

"Just a bit." Shit, what was wrong with me tonight? I can normally talk up a charming storm, especially with someone as cute as Robin. Instead I was reduced to monosyllables and not especially entertaining ones at that. "So tell me about your-self?" I decided to let him do the talking for a while. It would probably be a lot safer that way—and so it proved, because by the time we'd finished dessert, neither of us was in any doubt of where we were heading next. The only question was, whose room was the bed in?

Mine, It turned out. But not, I'm afraid, through choice. He paid the check, we finished our coffee, I stood, then stooped to pick up my purse—and the next thing I knew, I was flat on my back, alone in pitch darkness. I turned my head and the Indiglo numerals on the clock by my bed read *4:05*. I sat up, reached for where I knew the bedside lamp was and switched it on. Yes, my room, my bed. Someone had thoughtfully decided to remove a few of my clothes, but my bra and panties were still in place, and a blanket had obviously been pulled across me at some point.

Later, Robin told me that I'd blacked out in the restaurant; that the hotel doctor checked me out and declared it was probably a twenty-four-hour bug; then he and Robin carried me up to my room. "Best if she just sleeps it off," said the doc, and Robin, the sweetheart, said he'd stay there with me in case I woke up in the night and felt worse. I knew that bit already, though, because he was the next thing I saw, stretched out on the couch at the far end of the room, a book on his chest and fast asleep.

I sat watching him for a moment. The evening had been alive with promise...when he touched my hand, I swear I saw sparks, and when he took it and pressed it to his lips and murmured something that I only just heard (but I know the words "taste you" were in there somewhere), I almost wet myself there and then. In fact, now that I thought about it, the fact that I didn't wet myself should have warned me right away that I wasn't feeling quite right. Add that to my earlier inability to speak coherently, and maybe to the ease with which I fell asleep at the lecture, and the doctor was probably right. Maybe I did have a bug.

But I felt fine now. Finer than fine. I climbed out of bed and headed for the bathroom. Robin didn't stir, and I smiled at the bare feet protruding from beneath his blanket; smiled, too, as I spotted his trousers neatly folded on the chair, and his shirt carefully hung on the back.

I cleaned my teeth, peed, then stepped back into the room. He hadn't moved since I last passed, and I wondered about something: he'd left my underwear in place—what about his? I tiptoed to his side, crouched and lifted one corner of the blanket: long legs, hairy and muscular, and a pair of cotton briefs, good old-fashioned Y-fronts. Well, that answered that.

The thing is, there's a lot you can do with a pair of Y-fronts, especially if, like these, they're a little loose. For instance, using the tip of one finger, you can lift up one of the flaps and who knows what you'll find in there, all curled up and sleeping, just like its owner? And, if you're really careful, and you make sure to use your finger to gently roll it, rather than using your nail to hook it out, you can maneuver that something till it's just peeking out, still warm and unsuspecting. Then you can lean forward a little and stretch out your tongue...careful, don't jog him with your chin, just let him sleep on...and you just circle around that little slit with the tiniest tip of your tongue.

A story came to mind, one I'd read online a few nights before, about a girl who awakened her husband by sucking gently on his cock. What a wonderful way to greet a new day that must be. And it must be pretty good for the guy as well. I leaned forward a little closer and licked again. The taste on my tongue was tart but tantalizing as I danced lightly around that one closed eye, and this time I was rewarded with the merest hint of movement.

I glanced up at Robin's sleeping face. He lay impassive, completely unaware. But his dick knew something was going on, and as I ran my tongue once more across him, I could see it unfurling beneath the fabric of his briefs, thickening and strengthening, and pushing through the flap.

Boldly, I dragged my tongue across his helmet, then down onto the shaft. He wasn't fully erect yet—at best, he was semi-soft. But, even in the dim light cast by my bedside lamp, he was an impressive-looking fellow. I concentrated for a moment on that supersensitive spot, right where the helmet meets the shaft, and this time I got a twitch. And another one. *That's it, my beauty, just keep on hardening, and I'll do the rest.*

Flat on his back, Robin slept on. Was he dreaming, I wondered? And, if he was, was the state of his cock playing any part in it? I worked up a little spit and dribbled it onto his helmet. I blew gently. Another twitch and at last, his cock made its first attempt to rise, to reach out to whatever was teasing it so. A little more spit, a little more air, and this time...gotcha. His helmet was in my mouth, and I shuffled forward a little to inch my lips down his now rigid shaft.

I placed a finger between my legs and pressed against my panties, lightly stroking myself. For the first time, I thought about shaking him, but no. If Robin was going to awaken, then so be it. I wasn't going to give him any more help than I already was.

I sucked, gently and tentatively. He was still thickening; I could feel my jaw being pushed farther apart to accommodate his growing girth. I clamped my finger and thumb around the base of his shaft, holding him steady as I leaned in farther, feeling him sinking into my mouth, tapping the roof, nudging my throat. Then I moved back and forth, fucking him slowly, while my tongue lay flat on the bottom of my mouth, sending soft waves of motion against his flesh.

I had a rhythm, in my mouth and in my pussy—my finger was inside me now, stroking up toward my clitoris, circling around and then flitting away. I didn't want to come, not yet, and not like that. But I wanted to be ready for that moment when he did, and though I was sure that he was still asleep, I also knew that I would not be waiting long.

His hips were moving with me now, not violently or force-fully, but enough to let me know that more of his body was joining the party. My pinkie brushed his tight balls. They were huge, too, and I pictured myself trying to suck on them. It would have to be one at a time, but that was no hardship. It just gave me twice as much fun.

Precome on my tongue: I could taste it leaking now, sharp and maybe just a little too bitter. *Well, it's not a trip to Baskin-Robbins.* Robin, Robbins. I smiled at the synchronicity, but closed my mind to the rest of that thought. There's no law that says I have to swallow...hell, there's not even one that says he has to come in my mouth.

But isn't that half the fun of it? The salty shock, the liquid heat, the look in his eyes as I gulp down his muck...eyes I was suddenly conscious of, gazing down in shock and awe as my head bobbed down along his straining, stretching monster. And then he was pulling back, trying to draw away, and the faint moan that was escaping his lips was now stammering in panic:

"Shit, Chrissie, I'm coming...oh, god, here it comes!"

I was holding on fast, though, and I wasn't about to be cheated. Feeling his release and tasting it too—not so bad, after all, and a double scoop at least. I swallowed hard, feeling it thick and slick in my throat, and my own tensions were bursting in a wave that rushed up from the pit of my stomach to mix with the magic that was racing down from my throat. And I was still sucking, draining down the last drops, until I had to let go and fall flat on his lap, my breath hot and salty, my taste buds still dancing.

His hand was on my head. "Chrissie. That...you...were marvelous. Nobody's ever done that before. Not like that."

I couldn't resist a light tease. "Really? What did I do that was different?"

"You didn't stop." Hmmm, did I detect a faint stutter?

"Well, of course not. Should I have?"

"Other girls..." This was hard for him, and I silently chastised myself for making him spit it out. Or not. "Other girls say they don't like it."

"But how do they know if they've never done it with you?"

He was silent for a moment. "They tried it before, I guess."

"Well, they obviously did it wrong." I don't know, I've never understood those girls who'll go through life avoiding something, just because they didn't like it the first time. And then make a virtue out of it to a later lover, as though he really needs to know that he can't have what he wants, because some other guy got it first. Make up a lie, invent an excuse, tell him you want to save it for a special treat. But don't tell him that he cannot come in your mouth...or up your ass, or across your tits, or wherever else he might ask if he can do it...just because someone else did it first. That's not just rude, it's spiteful too, like him telling you he won't eat your cooking because his ex-wife's potatoes were hotter.

"Hey, what are you thinking about?" Robin's question burst into my mind.

"Oh, sorry." I shook my head. "Something a friend of mine was saying, about how more lovers lie about what we just did, than just about any other act there is."

Robin chuckled and ruffled my hair. "'I promise I won't come in your mouth.'"

I kissed his softness, felt it stir and raised it with a gentle fist. "Good," I said. "I'm glad to hear that." I lowered my head to suck on his helmet, then stopped and looked back up at him. "Oh, and yes, I'm feeling a lot better now. Thank you for asking."

"I kind of figured that out for myself," he said slowly. "And now, in the spirit of the absolute honesty with which we have apparently sworn to abide, please carry on with what you were just doing, or this time, I promise, I really *won't* come in your mouth."

I raised one hand and saluted smartly. "In that case, maybe I'll come in yours." And he was already reaching for my hips before I'd even finished my sentence.

HOLE IN YOUR POCKET

Donna George Storey

Does every woman have a man like this in her life?

You step into the classroom on the first day of your first seminar, and your eyes are immediately drawn to him. You hear a little *Oh, my* in your head and spend the rest of the afternoon shooting quick glances in his direction. He grins at you, and your stomach does a flip. After a few collegial chats in the history department's student lounge, however, you learn he's engaged to someone back home, not that you're ready to settle down with anyone yourself. Not even a slim young man with honey hair, sapphire eyes and a smile like the first day of summer vacation.

You quickly become "friends." The two of you take long walks around campus as veils of orange and pink and violet trail across the western sky. You always feel smarter and prettier around him. You talk about everything, even things you don't tell your new boyfriend who just wouldn't understand. Sometimes he tells you about his fiancée, and you always do your best to sound respectful, even in awe, of their beautiful relationship. You notice he doesn't smile quite as much when you talk about your boyfriend, unless you're complaining a little, then he hints, diplomatically, that you deserve the best in life and should never settle for less.

In all that time you never do anything more than hug, hugs that never last long enough because you want to float in the heat of his arms and take all sustenance solely from his delicious scent of cumin and shampoo. Even the bristle of his five o'clock shadow on your cheek feels like the finest velvet. You're dreading his wedding, but you go anyway because he'd be hurt if you didn't. His wife is prettier than you are by all common measures—her hair is blonder, her breasts are bigger, her legs are longer—but somehow you sense the marriage won't last. You tell yourself it's your own jealousy and vow to stop lusting after a married man.

He moves to D.C. to take a job teaching modern European history at Georgetown, and you lose touch for a while. But then, a couple of years later, you run into each other at a conference. You stay up until three in the morning in an Irish bar drinking and talking like the years have melted away. You begin to email regularly—chatty notes about work, politics, the meaning of history. It's all very safe and intellectual, but your pulse still jumps when you see his name in your in-box.

The next time you "happen" to be drinking into the wee hours at a conference, he admits things haven't been going well with his wife for some time, and they've decided to separate. You feel sad for him even if you get to be right.

When he finds out he didn't get tenure, you're the first person he calls. He claims it's a gift. *I've spent my whole fucking life doing what other people told me to do and now I'm done with it. Fuck it. Fuck it all.*

You think, with a smile, that you wish he'd put you on the list of things to fuck, too. That night you masturbate to your usual fantasy about him. You're in a tiny room together, the size of a small closet. Inside it's dark and humid, but you can hear the chatter and music of a fancy party right outside the door. He pins you to the wall and makes love to you right there, his dick skewering you so hard you're forced up on your toes. You can't make a sound to show your pleasure or you'll be caught, humiliated, shamed before the respectable people outside. You bite back your cries in real life, too, and the orgasm is so intense, tears of pleasure roll down your cheeks. Then you lick your salty fingers and imagine it's his come.

In June he calls and says he's taking a whole year off just to figure out his life. He's always wanted to travel to Asia, in no small part because of your interest in the area. It just so happens he'll be spending one night in San Francisco on his way to Tokyo. He asks if you'll be around, and without thinking, you insist he stay at your place.

But then you reconsider. It's a dangerous combination, the two of you alone in your apartment, both of you free. One glass of wine and you'll probably make a fool of yourself, confess your sick "imprisoned in the closet" fantasy, or brush your lips tellingly against his cheek when you give him a "friendly" hug good night. And then he'll know what you've been dreaming of all along. He'll pity you for it.

You curl up on your guest room futon, where he'll be sleeping in one short week, and give yourself a good pep talk. You imagine a golden veil around his whole body, a barrier that will protect the purity of your friendship forever. Because part of the pleasure of your secret lust is that you have never fucked him and never will. That's why your relationship is so perfect.

Confident in your motives, you clean every inch of your

apartment and prepare your signature "scattered sushi" platter and homemade green-tea ice cream. He always praised your offerings at the department potlucks back in the old days.

The doorbell rings.

Your heart is hammering, but you force yourself to glide to the door like a queen.

The sight of him in your doorway is like a punch to the solar plexus. He is thinner than when you last saw him, and his cheeks show a day's growth of travel-weary blond beard. But he is so gleamingly gorgeous in the summer dusk, the words of friendly greeting catch in your throat.

He steps forward and wraps you in his arms.

You are totally enveloped in his warm, muscular embrace, his dizzying male scent. He doesn't pull away. You immediately understand this is not the usual hug.

Yes.

You could be the one to pull back but you tighten your arms around him instead, and he moans, a faintly mournful sound. He squeezes you harder still as if he'll crush you. You think of that hot little room in your brain where he fucks and fucks and fucks you up against the wall until your knees turn to hot butterscotch.

Your legs are already melting.

You aren't exactly surprised when his lips find yours. His whiskers scrape your chin and cheeks, but the punishment excites you. You immediately open your mouth to his tongue, sucking him deep inside like a cock.

Yes.

You kiss like teenagers, tongues twirling and sparring, as if you're afraid you'll be forced to stop. This isn't supposed to be happening, and yet how absurdly easy it is to slip over the line. It's like the time you found a hole in the pocket of your jeans at a party. Your finger slipped right through, and you couldn't help but take advantage of the secret entrance to tickle the sensitive flesh of your inner thigh with your fingertip. You pulled your hand out guiltily, but soon found an excuse to go to the powder room where you forced open the entire pocket with your fist then masturbated and watched yourself come in the vanity mirror.

You've always been the kind of woman who makes the best of circumstances.

That's when you pull away. He looks confused. You laugh and take his hand and drag him to your bedroom, knowing now he won't pity you, quite the contrary. You fall onto the mattress together, and you're kissing again, mouths wide as if you're devouring each other's face. Haven't you've both been starving for this for ten long years? The heat and pressure of his hard-on against you is the sweetest feeling you've ever known.

He wants me, he wants me, he wants me.

Both of you are whimpering and panting. Four hands fumble with buttons and zippers. He has you naked before you're even done with his belt, but you surrender gracefully, pressing your bare breasts against his hot chest. You're in the middle of your cycle, which means you're horny as hell and your nipples are exquisitely sensitive, already throbbing, and he hasn't even touched them yet.

You're so drunk with lust, your fingers are clumsy at his zipper. Finally he yanks down his own pants and kicks them to the floor impatiently. One hand disappears over the bed. You sneak a peek at his cock, which is a good length and thick and very red. He holds up a condom in its wrapper, smiling like he's won a prize.

"That's not from your wallet, is it?" you blurt out, then regret it. Even one word might destroy this magic, draw you back into the ordinary world.

"I bought it at the drugstore on the way over. Was it too forward of me?"

Up close, his eyes are seawater blue flecked with gray. Your reply is a laugh, and you fling yourself against him.

The first time you fuck that night, he's on top. Old-fashioned, yes, but you pretend it's your wedding night, centuries ago, when some couples were betrothed for years and years until the man had made his way in the world enough to support a lady in the manner to which she was accustomed. Of course, by that measure, he's come down in the world, but you like that, too. If he weren't between lives, he wouldn't be here, with you, naked and touchable. You spread your legs and sigh as he slides inside, his shaft massaging that ancient ache inside your belly. You fit together well this way. You move together well, too. There's something liquid about the way your hips undulate in unison. His wiry blond hair down there chafes your clit just the right way, a prickling pleasure. He's nipping and tweaking your nipples as you fuck, and it drives you crazy, the pleasure hovering on the knife's edge of pain. You're going to come soon—too soon?—but you sense that won't be the end of this crazy time out of time.

It's never like this your first time with a new lover; you're always too nervous; but with him, well, haven't you been dancing around in a teasing, masochistic kind of foreplay since you first met? His merciless lips on your nipples are just a reminder of that sweet suffering. You hook your feet around his thighs and grind your clit harder up against his belly. That's all it takes. You explode with a scream around his cock, and he sucks your tit hard until your spasms stop, and then he croons your name and with an *Oh, god, oh, god* his hips drive into you. Your own body shudders as he releases into you. You realize that's what you really wanted all these years, to feel him come in your arms.

Afterward you're a little afraid to look at him, but he pulls you close and gazes steadily into your eyes and says, "That was so amazing. Even better than I imagined."

His expression is so pleased, you feel like you're looking into a mirror.

"Did you *imagine*?" you ask.

"More than I should admit. Did you ever...?" There's a touching uncertainty in his voice.

"You know we've always had so much in common." You laugh and nestle together for a while, and then you say, "Hey, are you hungry?"

He nods and you slip on his shirt without asking because you like the smell of him around you. Besides it means he'll have to go shirtless, and you like to look at his chest. He smiles and squeezes your naked ass under the shirttails.

You have a picnic on your living room floor—cold sake and sushi rice scattered with strips of raw fish, sweet omelet and pickled lotus root. You talk about sunny things, his plans for his trip, the new female-centered history course you're developing which is sure to change the world. After you're finished eating, he pulls you on top of him and asks hopefully if you're the dessert. He slides his hands under his shirt and cups your breasts, and before you know it, you're straddling him and rocking your wet cunt into his hard belly. You feel his erection brushing your ass, and you get a wicked idea. You tell him to wait and rush to the kitchen for the green-tea ice cream. First you feed him some with a spoon. Then he wants to rub some on your nipples, and you let him. The chill both soothes and arouses the tender tips. Finally you unveil your trick—you take a mouthful and go down on him. He squirms and laughs, but his dick gets harder in your mouth.

You wrap your fist around his sticky tool and show off all

of your skills, tonguing him right below the head, squeezing your lips around him as if to milk him dry. That is in fact your goal, to drive him wild so he shoots his special cream down your throat.

"I want to come inside you, please, stop," he begs.

You pull off and give him your best dominatrix glare. "If you come in my mouth like a good boy, you can fuck me all night long in any way you want."

You can almost see the wheels spinning in his head. Eyes narrowed, he lies back and submits.

Even with his naked cock in your mouth, you can't believe this is so easy. He was the one man you could never have for as long as your body can remember, and suddenly you can touch him and taste him anywhere you please. And what you want more than anything now is this, his salty dick pressing into your throat. You suck him like you've never sucked anyone, and the weirdest thing is you feel him *down there*, too, filling you, satisfying you like food.

His thighs tremble and his cock grows impossibly hard. Your lips register the spasms first, then jets of jism shoot up against your palate. He is sweeter than you expected, the grassy taste of him blending perfectly with the lingering flavor of astringent green tea.

He doesn't let you gloat over your achievement for long. He pushes you down and rolls you over and yanks your knees open. For a moment, you're afraid, but then you feel something cool and smooth along your asscrack—his fingers rubbing melted ice cream there. You start to laugh, but it fades into a moan when he starts to lick you. You've let guys fuck your ass, but no one's ever enjoyed your back door with such gusto. His finger snakes up to strum your clit, and suddenly your whole body is melting under his hot tongue. You start to beg him to fuck you, but decide, in the little corner of your head that can still think, that this is better. You want him to take one of your virginities. If he makes you come while he's tonguing your ass, that part of your pleasure will be his forever.

In the shadows of night, it's easier to talk about sad things. He tells you he hasn't had a blow job in years, and yours felt so good, the best he's ever had. You confess no one's ever licked your ass, and you like it more than you ever thought you would, even if it makes you a pervert. After that you simply lie in each other's arms in silence.

Then he whispers that he wants to do something else for you, something no one's ever done before. That's when you tell him about the closet fantasy. Scholar that he is, he admires the perfect symbolism: the dark, secret hideaway; the disapproving public right outside the door. He asks you how big your closet is. You tell him "big enough."

He's rough when he pushes you up against the wall, trapping you with his hard, feverish body. Yet his lips are tender, almost teasing. He kisses your forehead, your cheeks, your ears, your neck. All the while his cock presses against your belly, and you hope somehow it will leave a permanent mark on the skin.

You whimper and push your hips against him and he calls you "impatient" and tells you he'll fuck you soon enough. He pinches your nipples steadily, and the flaming sensation shoots straight to your cunt, until your thighs are shamefully slippery with sweat and juice. At last he crouches slightly and starts to probe your slit with the head of his sheathed cock. You push up on tiptoe and tilt your pelvis forward so he can reach the hole. He slides in. The sensation is so very different from any other coupling, as if you're straddling a pole, riding it. His shaft pushes up against your clit, rubbing it with each thrust. Your legs start to wobble and shake. You're gasping and moaning and he's growling in your ear what a pervert you are for liking it so much, fucking up against a wall like a street whore. It's a risky thing to say, but it's exactly what you want to hear. It's the words as much as his cock that makes you come—very loudly. He starts to plow you before your orgasm fades. Again your secret flesh spasms in sympathy as he comes into you, grimacing and grunting.

You lean against each other, laughing softly and so damned proud of yourselves. It's past midnight and without another word you both collapse onto your bed. When you wake up, it's dawn. You lie there and watch him sleep for a long time. Strangely, he seems most yours now, even more than when you had him wrapped in your arms and legs and cunt. You think of that hole in your pocket, and how you sewed it up after your night of selfish pleasure because it was your favorite pair of jeans. You still have them in your drawer, although you don't wear them much anymore.

The last twelve hours were a gift of pure magic. You know the end will be magic, too. The moment he wakes, the hole will mend itself. The golden veil of purity will descend. But for now you steal this moment to gaze at his face and wonder how one person can give you so much pain and pleasure all at the same time.

You smile when it hits you that after this night, the pleasure will always outweigh the pain.

MAID SERVICE

Jan Darby

No one ever aspired to be a maid when she grew up, Allison Ferreira thought as she pushed her cart down the hallway of the Suite Spot. Everyone wanted to be a lawyer or a doctor or a CEO, not the woman who tidied up after them. But that was about the only job available after she'd fallen off her career ladder. She'd taken it, just as an interim thing, to buy herself some time to figure out what she really wanted to do.

A few minutes later, Allison had just finished making the bed in Room 402, and was placing the finishing touch—the hotel's trademark "suite sweet"—on the pillow, when she heard the door opening. She'd only been working here for three days, but one of the first rules she'd been taught was that she was supposed to be invisible to the guests, like a guardian angel, taking care of their every need, without ever being seen.

Allison moved as unobtrusively as possible toward the exit, keeping her eyes focused on the carpet. As she was about to pass him, she murmured a soft "Excuse me."

"For what?" The sincere curiosity in his voice startled her into looking him directly in the face, something she knew was forbidden. He wasn't the most beautiful man she'd ever seen, or the ugliest either. He looked like every other tired sales rep who stayed at the Suite Spot, passing through on his way to the next small town in his route, the next sales call. His eyes were different, though. They sparkled with the same curiosity that she'd noticed in his voice.

"I'm sorry about being here in your room," she said.

"You shouldn't be," he said. "It saves me from having to call housekeeping."

"What do you need?"

"I haven't decided." He dropped his sample case on the small desk in the corner. "What's available?"

"I've got spare towels and toiletries and coffee supplies on my cart," she said. "That's about it. Except for the suite sweets, of course. I could get you another one."

"I've never had much of a sweet tooth." He glanced at the pillow where the exquisitely handmade, dark-chocolate rose lay. "What about you?"

"I adore chocolate." And the custom-made roses were a particular favorite: extra-dark, extra-premium, extra-decadent. She'd received one—a damaged one, not good enough for a guest, but too good to throw out—on the day she'd been hired. It was probably the one and only perk she'd ever get from this job, but that was okay, since she wasn't planning to be here for long. A couple months, at the most. Just until she found something better. Or maybe she could go back to school and get another degree.

"You can have mine, if you want."

"No, thank you," she said automatically, but she couldn't help glancing at the rose. The management didn't care if the staff took home the occasional shampoo bottle, but they had strict rules about the roses, and taking one without permission, even an imperfect or damaged one, was grounds for immediate dismissal. She might not be planning to stay for long, but she needed this job until she found a better one.

"I wasn't thinking properly," he said. "You've probably had a hundred of them and would prefer something different for a change."

She took another step away from him, toward the exit, like the good little maid she'd been hired to be. His curiosity about her was too appealing, though, and she couldn't make herself avert her eyes from his. He didn't try to prevent her from leaving, but she got the distinct impression that he was disappointed almost as much as she was, at the thought that she'd never get to know anything about him. Anything that mattered, at least. He would remain a stranger, just one among the dozens of guests she would run across every week. She doubted she'd even remember him by tomorrow when another tired sales rep checked into this room.

"I'm..." She hesitated. Management had another rule, even stricter than the one about the roses, and it prohibited fraternizing with guests. "I'm Cheri." The lie probably wouldn't save her job if he reported her, but it did give her plausible deniability.

"Jeremy." He crossed the room to pick up the chocolate rose by its lollipop stem and hold it out to her.

She shook her head.

"Oh, come on," he said. "It's just a fancy sucker. It's not like I'm propositioning you."

"I can't touch it or I'll be fired."

He tossed it back onto the bed. "Damn. I was hoping you'd stick around and we could talk for a while, maybe share something from room service."

She would have liked that too, but she had to be careful.

"*I* can't touch the rose. The rule, and I quote, is 'chocolate is for the guests' use only.' It doesn't say anything about how you use it. Or with whom."

Jeremy blinked, but it didn't take more than a fraction of a second for him to catch on, and he lunged for the king-sized bed to retrieve the chocolate. Once he had it, though, he paused, turning the rose's stem thoughtfully.

Finally, he flopped on the bed, propping himself against the headrest, messing up the pillows she'd so recently fluffed. He tore off a small strip of the decorative red foil from the tip of the rose and bent his head slightly to smell the chocolate. "Good stuff. Not that I'm an expert, of course."

He licked the exposed tip, and she felt it as if he'd licked her nipples. "Really good stuff."

She swallowed.

"Want some?" he said.

She nodded.

"I've always wondered why people were so fascinated with chocolate," he said, watching her intently.

"The scientists say it's because of hormones," she said. "Chocolate causes the body to release serotonin into the bloodstream."

"I suppose that could be it," he said. "But there are other hormones. Other releases that are pleasurable."

She shrugged, as if she hadn't noticed the reference to orgasm. She'd been warned that guests might proposition her. It was a natural consequence of the guests being away from home, lonely and bored. She was supposed to ignore any such innuendos and retreat as quickly as possible. There was even an official form for reporting such behavior, as if the proposition were some sort of work-related accident. What they hadn't warned her about was the possibility that she might be inclined to proposition the guest.

He licked the chocolate rose again. "I just don't get it. Why choose chocolate instead of some other pleasure?"

She knew what she was supposed to say—something noncommittal, and then steer him back to the things that the hotel offered: extra pillows, blankets or chocolate. Except that wasn't what either of them wanted.

She took a step closer to the bed. "It doesn't have to be a choice. A person could have both."

His eyes lit up. "I don't want both. I want you."

Her pussy clenched in response. She wanted both, but only on her own terms. She'd been a formidable negotiator in her previous career. "I still want the chocolate."

"One taste," he said. "And then I get to taste you."

She leaned down and licked the rose he was holding, moaning just a little at the extraordinary quality.

He pulled the chocolate away, out of her lips' reach. "My turn."

She pulled the hotel-logo sport shirt over her head and removed her bra, a little self-conscious about how plain it was, compared to the shiny red foil encasing the chocolate rose.

He didn't seem to care. He licked her breasts exactly as she'd done to the rose, complete with an appreciative moan for each nipple. She could see him struggle with the urge to keep on licking, but after a moment, he leaned back against the pillows.

"Do you have sex with all the male guests?"

"No." He didn't need to know he was the first guest she'd even talked to. For the moment, she wasn't Allison, the temporary housekeeper; she was Cheri, the adventurous maid. "Just the ones who know what a woman wants."

He raised the rose to her mouth, pressing it between her lips. As soon as her tongue touched the chocolate, his mouth was on her nipple. She sucked the candy, and he sucked her. She licked greedily, but without taking an actual bite, hoping to prolong the pleasure for both of them. Still, the chocolate melted down to the edge of the foil wrapper, and she couldn't get to the rest of the treat without his assistance. She pulled away from him a little, and he copied her action.

"The wrapper," she said, nodding toward the rose. "I can't eat the rest until the foil is gone."

He ran the rose down the side of her neck, between her breasts and toward the waistband of her khaki pants, leaving a trail of chocolate behind. "There's too much covering you too. I want to see the rest of you."

She immediately tugged down the bottom half of her uniform. He unwrapped the rose slowly, pausing as her panties were revealed, and then again when her panties were gone. She gestured impatiently at the last scrap of foil at the base of the rose, and he absently removed it without taking his gaze off her.

He reached toward her pussy, apparently unaware that he was holding the rose until it brushed against her thigh. He looked up, following the trail of chocolate that started at the spot where her waistband had been, all the way to her mouth, which was salivating for more—of the candy and of him.

"Is this what you want?" He waved the chocolate in front of her face.

She caught the scent of it and started to reach for it with her lips. He moved it away then, slowly, tantalizingly just out of reach, until she was bent over him, while he lay sprawled across the bed. Her hands were locked behind her back so she wouldn't forget and reach for the forbidden treat. Her breasts dangled directly over his face as she tried to capture the elusive chocolate.

"Luscious," he said, and began sucking her breasts again.

She managed to get her mouth on the chocolate, despite her precarious position over him. This time she gave in to the greed and bit the remaining chocolate off its stem.

He released his lips' hold on her breast and said, "Hey, no fair. You got the whole thing before I finished my treat."

She closed her eyes and savored the still-melting chocolate, unable to speak with her mouth full.

"You aren't finished, though, are you?" he said.

She shook her head.

He took her hand to pull her down onto the bed beside him, but she resisted.

"You aren't allowed to lie down on the job, I bet."

She nodded.

"No problem." He maneuvered her into a kneeling position, straddling his chest, with her pussy directly in front of his face. He stuck a pillow behind his head and began to lick her pussy with as much determination as she'd shown in capturing the rose.

She moaned.

"Was the chocolate as good as that felt?"

She could still taste the lingering remnants of the dark, decadent chocolate. "Yes."

"I'll have to try harder then." His tongue found its way to her clit and began a flicking motion that weakened her muscles. She sank onto his chest, and he stopped.

"You're not allowed to sit on the job," he said. "I can't suck you from this angle."

With an effort, she rose above him again, giving him full access. Her muscles quivered along the inside of her thighs and inside her pussy. "I can't wait much longer."

"You promised me," he said. "You had your treat, and now it's my turn. I don't eat anything all in one gulp like you." He closed his mouth on her clit and sucked once. "I like to savor everything. Make it last and last and last."

"I can't."

"Yes, you can." He placed his hands on her hips and then slid them down beneath her ass, supporting her, holding her in place. "Tell me what you like."

"I like chocolate."

He gave her clit a lick.

"I like this."

"Me too." He resumed sucking, slowly, persistently and eagerly.

She squirmed, she wiggled, she clenched, responding to his implicit curiosity about what felt best to her. He held her in place as he pursued his gastronomic experiments, adjusting his speed and pressure and then waiting to see how she responded.

And she did respond. He would soon have all the answers he could ever want.

He paused to ask, "How much time do we have?"

"Not long," she said. "Another few seconds, and I'm going to come."

"And after that?" While he waited for her answer, he fingered her clit.

She gasped, but managed to say, "All night. My shift just ended, but I don't need to leave. You can have me until checkout."

"The chocolate was that good?"

"No," she said. "You're that good. I need more of you."

"Me too." He found her clit again with his mouth and sucked until she was shaking with the effort to remain upright.

Finally, either he realized she couldn't last any longer, or his own curiosity about her orgasm won out over his self-control. She shuddered with the pleasure of breaking just about every rule in the management's handbook, including the unwritten one about never, ever, ever fucking the guests.

Some time later, after they'd broken a few more rules, and his curiosity, along with his cock, was finally satisfied, he said, "I'll be sure to let your supervisor know that you gave me the best maid service I've ever had." He rolled her beneath him and pillowed his face on her breasts.

She suspected there would be additional rule-breaking before the night was over, and if she weren't already so drained, she would have shivered in anticipation. For the moment, she simply enjoyed his closeness and contemplated the benefits of her job. Sure, the housekeeping work itself was pretty dull. But tonight had been exciting. Tonight's interlude with a stranger, someone she knew virtually nothing about, someone she'd never see again, had been better than anything she'd felt with her more long-term lovers.

It dawned on her that with the number of guests passing through the Suite Spot, she could have this same kind of intense excitement whenever she wanted it, whenever she let herself be caught inside an appealing guest's room.

Allison hugged Jeremy closer, grateful not just for the pleasure they'd shared, but also for the way he'd helped her see the truth about her job. Until now, she'd been as shortsighted as everyone else, never even considering a career as a maid. For too many years, she'd been working her way up the traditional corporate ladder, fighting for job perks she hadn't even cared about. Here at the Suite Spot, there was no ladder to climb, and the only job perks were the ones she created for herself.

Jeremy started licking her breasts again, and Allison sighed with the pleasure. She didn't want to be a doctor or a lawyer or a CEO. She wanted to be a maid. With benefits.

CHASING JARED

Heidi Champa

My cell phone beeped, the tinny electronic sound mixing in with the din of the people in the office. As much as I wanted to look at it right away, the computer screen in front of me and the voice on my landline were demanding my attention. As soon as I could break free from actual work, I picked up my iPhone and brought up the screen I had been waiting for. That much-anticipated beep signaled the presence of the best food truck in town: Jared's Bad-Ass Cheeseburgers.

I had fallen in love with the burgers the very first time I tasted one. I had never really been a fan of hamburgers: too many bad memories of burnt patties from family barbeques. These were not your run-of-the-mill hamburgers. It very well might have been the best food I had ever put in my mouth. The burger itself was magical enough. But, Jared, the incredibly hot guy who ran the food truck, didn't just do plain old burgers. Each one was a masterpiece of flavors, made to order and served with just a few thick-cut fries.

Since that first taste all those months ago, I had been stalking Jared and his burgers using a specialized application on my phone. It would alert me to Jared's proximity to both my home and office. I had gotten lucky a few times, the truck showing up at just the right time, the burgers falling right into my lap like a little slice of heaven. Those were the best days. But, most of the time, like now, I couldn't just drop everything I was doing and run out into the street to get a burger. As much as I wanted to, I was trapped behind my desk, and I would have to forgo one of Jared's burgers for yet another day. I set my phone down and sighed, turning back to the report that remained unfinished on my computer screen.

It wasn't only Jared's burgers that had me so drawn to that silver and black food truck, practically turning me into a psycho stalker. The man himself kept me coming back for more. The other thing my smart phone was really good for: finding out more information about our local celebrity chef. I devoured information about him as readily as I ate up his food creations, desperate to know more about him. My obsession grew every time he served me, his dark eyes piercing me through the truck window. His smile made me melt faster than his twenty varieties of cheese did on those smoking-hot burgers. The tattoos that covered his muscled forearms were almost too much for me to bear.

I started wearing low-cut tops every time I visited Jared, because the height of the food truck meant he would get the chance to look down my shirt. I caught him doing just that a few times, and the thrill of it kept me buzzing for the rest of the day. I never really talked to Jared, other than to place my order. I would form whole conversations with him in my head, but I always chickened out at the last minute, choosing instead to focus on my burger and casting a stray glance his way as

I ate. On the plus side, I had visited Jared's truck so often he seemed to remember me. Or, at least, he remembered my order. That had to count for something. Secretly, I wished for him to make the first move, but that hardly seemed practical, given that every time I saw him he was working at an intense pace. My desire continued to grow from afar; every wink, smile and accidental touch throwing another log on the fire inside me. Just like the double jalapeño burger I loved to order.

My phone had been strangely silent for days. I checked it a million times, just to make sure the thing was still functional. I worried at first that I had finally dropped it one too many times, but everything was still working properly. Jared had seemingly disappeared off the map, the app I had no longer giving me the information I so craved. I expanded the search area to include the areas I had never bothered to go to and I found him, all the way across town, serving burgers miles and miles away from me. That bastard. How could he forsake me like that?

I was pissed. Not just because it had been way too long since I'd savored one of his fabulous burgers. I missed him, in a weird way. This was a guy I barely spoke to, but he had become such a part of my consciousness, it was hard not having him close at hand. I didn't want to have to drive so many miles to satisfy my urges, both for him and for food. Resigned, I tried to forget about him and his stupid truck, even going so far as to eat burgers from other places. But they paled in comparison, never quite scratching my itch the way Jared could. I had given up hope, but every time I thought about dumping the food truck app from my phone, something stopped me. I just couldn't turn my back on him completely.

I was jonesing hard very late one night, almost to the point where I was ready to drive to the twenty-four-hour market and try to duplicate Jared's magic in my own kitchen. About to settle instead for the leftover Chinese food in my fridge, I paused when I heard a familiar sound coming from the depths of my purse. It couldn't be, could it? I practically ran across the room, digging in my bag like a wild woman, hoping against hope that it wasn't just some pointless text message from a friend or a bill reminder from my service provider. When I looked at the pristine flat screen, I saw the flashing red light I had been waiting to see for weeks. Jared was back and just a few blocks away.

Throwing on whatever clothes I could find, I charged into my car, racing to the spot where my crush and my burger were waiting for me. My car was the only one on the street, and I was so relieved when I noticed that Jared's truck had no one standing in front of it. In fact, we were the only two people on the road at that moment, the city quiet for a change. It took every ounce of strength I possessed not to run screaming toward that black and silver oasis, choosing instead to walk as casually as I could to my destiny. My breath caught as I saw Jared busily working behind the slightly steamy windows. He looked up and saw me, his smile nearly making me turn and run. But, I pressed on, taking each step slowly as I made my way to the truck's order window.

I opened my mouth to speak, but Jared beat me to the punch.

"Hey there, stranger. Haven't seen you in a while. Let me guess, double jalapeño burger with extra cheese."

I don't know why I hesitated, the word *yes* was just a breath away, but for some reason I just stood silent in front of him, letting his eyes roam over me. I took one more step closer, the metal counter right underneath my chin. I stared up into his eyes, letting the delicious smell coming from inside the truck waft into my nose. Finally, I managed to find my words.

"Not tonight. I'm thinking I should try something different. Something a little adventurous. What do you recommend?"

He smiled like a mischievous schoolboy, wiping his hands on a heavily stained rag. Picking up a silver bowl, he dipped a spoon into it and offered it to me. I opened my mouth without thinking, letting the cool metal spoon slip between my lips. The flavors exploded on my tongue, spicy and sweet mixing to perfection as I swallowed the cool liquid down my throat. I put my hand on his to steady the spoon as he pulled away, touching him for the first time. The combination sent a shock down my spine and made me just a little wet.

"It's delicious. What is it?"

"Just a new sauce I've been working on. I thought you might like it. I started using it last week. It's a shame you haven't been around in a while."

"Well, you haven't been on this side of town in a while."

"And, how do you know that? Are you having me followed?"

"Not exactly, Jared."

I blushed, not wanting to admit that I was basically stalking him electronically. I just shrugged, refusing to embarrass myself any further.

"Well, you're right. I haven't been over in this part of town for a while. I'm trying to expand the business a little. But I didn't forget about you, Celia."

I must have looked shocked, as I had no idea he remembered my name. He had never used it before. He crossed those tattooed arms over his chest, the black shirt he was wearing streaked with sauces and spices. Suddenly, the last thing on my mind was a burger. All I could think about was how those strong hands would feel on my body. But I had to at least pretend I was just there for the food. After all, I truly did want both.

"So, can I get a burger with that new sauce, Jared?"

This time he hesitated, standing stock-still as he seemed to process my request. He finally started moving, cooking and constructing my burger as I watched. He placed the gorgeous creation into a container, but instead of handing it out the window to me, he just set it aside, leaning down to look me in the eye instead.

"Can I have my burger now, Jared?"

"Sure, sure. In a minute. But I thought you said you were looking for some adventure tonight, Celia. I don't think you're really after just a burger tonight, are you? I think you want something more than that. In fact, I think you've wanting something more from that very first day. Well, am I right, Celia?"

My throat had completely dried up, but I managed to shake my head yes. For the first time ever, I was standing in front of that black and silver truck and the last thing on earth I wanted was that amazing-looking burger he'd just made.

Jared didn't need any more encouragement; he set about closing the order windows and drawing the small shades that covered them. I heard him unlatch the small door at the back of the truck. I practically ran around to it, moving quickly up the two small steps that led into the makeshift kitchen. My heart was pounding, my fingers beginning to tingle at the thought of what was about to happen. I looked around the shiny interior of the truck, the tiny space filled to the brim with cooking supplies, food and a comically large grill.

Before I could do another thing, Jared had me in his arms, his lips on mine. It was the exact thing I had wanted to do but had been too timid to manage on my own. Thank god for Jared's forcefulness. He tasted like a mixture of his secret sauce and beer; clearly he'd been sneaking a few during the late-night hours.

My hands dug into his strong back, clutching on to him as he moved me toward an empty counter near the front of the truck. Hitched up onto the counter, our mouths still connected, I wrapped my legs around his back. His hands ran up my back, one hand wrapping securely in my hair. With my neck exposed, Jared went in for the kill, nipping at it with little bites. Each one made me gasp; the way he mixed pleasure and pain was yet another perfect concoction.

Moving on quickly, as if we were both starving, he yanked my shirt over my head, leaving me bare, as I hadn't bothered with a bra. I tore his T-shirt from his body, tossing it aside with haste. I pulled him back to me, wanting another taste of his mouth. I also took a moment to admire his chest, more tattoos now exposed. He dropped to his knees in front of me, the thud echoing through the metal box of the truck, making quick work of the button and zipper on my jeans.

I was naked before I knew it, the metal counter cold on my ass, but his large hands pushing my thighs apart felt hot. He tugged me forward on the counter, until my naked cunt was right in front of his face. I looked down at him, hardly able to believe that all my stalking had finally paid off. Jared licked his thick lips, dragging a thumb over my swollen clit, toying with me for just a moment before he lowered those moist lips to my slit. I let my head fall back, careful not to crush the bags of buns that were on the shelf behind me. Jared's tongue swirled circles over and around my clit, a thick finger dipping inside me.

I clutched at his head, keeping him close, grinding my hips into his face as he wrapped his lips around my clit and sucked hard. I moaned in the small space, the echo catching me off guard. Two fingers fucked me, my cunt clenching around him each time he entered. He pulled away, his thumb replacing his tongue on my clit, his eyes meeting mine. His face was still wet with my juices, his eyes focused with desire. His words shocked me, made me want him even more.

"You taste amazing. I should put you on the menu."

His fingers pushed and pulled, twisting slightly as he fucked me slowly. His other hand reached up and teased my hard nipple, adding a pinch of hurt to the bliss he was serving me. I steadied myself on the counter, suddenly feeling very close to the edge, literally and figuratively. Jared stood up, shucking his pants off, pausing long enough to retrieve a condom from his pocket. My eyes went straight to his cock, which stood at attention, the thick length of him making my mouth water.

I moved to get off the counter, but he stopped me, clearly wanting me just where I was. I reached out and snatched the condom from him, tearing it open with my teeth. I took his cock in my hand, jerking him, enjoying the feel of him. Part of me wanted to take my time, torture him a little, but it was beyond me at that point. I rolled the condom down, my hands trembling just a bit. He wrapped a hand around my neck, kissing me roughly. I moaned into his mouth as he entered me, his thick cock spreading me open. He stayed still for a few moments, our eyes meeting, before he started to pull back out.

I could actually feel the truck starting to rock as he fucked me, my legs once again around his back. The thought of the giant black and silver truck swaying made a small giggle bubble up in my throat, but Jared swallowed the sound with another kiss, pulling on my bottom lip with his teeth. I hung on to him for dear life; the muscles of his shoulders were tense under my fingers. Jared was grunting and so was the truck, its creaking axles keeping perfect time to our frantic pace. His forehead rested against mine as he began to slow down, easing us back from the brink. He took my hand, guiding it between our bodies until my fingers were right above my clit.

My fingers slid over the swollen nub, but he was controlling my every move, matching our tempos. It was so intense I could barely stand it, the last of my resolve slipping away. I don't know how I did it, but I managed to speak. Well, sort of.

"Jared, please."

He smiled, just for a second, before kissing me again, pressing my fingers harder against my clit. That last bit of pressure was all it took to push me over the edge, my orgasm slamming into me like a freight train. I could no longer keep my eyes open, my pussy clamping down on his cock, Jared moving my fingers so quickly I could hardly keep up. Throwing my head back, I screamed, the metal walls bouncing the sound all around us, my free hand still squeezing his shoulder. I could barely breathe, my lungs struggling for each gasp of air. Jared released my hand, grabbing on to my hips as he pounded into me furiously, coming hard just as I was finishing, his powerful thrusts pushing me back on the counter until the shelves were digging into my back.

Suddenly, everything stopped. The truck stopped swaying and Jared and I were quiet. He kissed me, first on my sweaty forehead and then on my lips. We straightened ourselves out, cleaning up the mess we had just made. Jared and I stood facing each other, just a few feet apart in the tiny space. I didn't know what to say, but I should have known that Jared would.

"Sorry, but I think your burger is cold by now."

"It's no problem Jared. I'm sure it will still taste amazing."

"Just like you."

He kissed me, pressing the Styrofoam container into my hands. I left the truck, and as soon as I got back to my car, Jared pulled away into the night. I watched the black and silver truck disappear over the hill. That night, I feasted on the best burger I'd ever had, the new sauce even better than I expected it to be. Jared managed to satisfy me again that night, without even being there.

Soon after that night, Jared turned in his big, beautiful truck for a head chef gig at a fancy restaurant downtown. The place became so popular, it was nearly impossible to get a table. I hear the burgers are fantastic.

BREATHING

Daniel Burnell

The first thing, if you were me, was that you didn't want to seem needy. Second, you didn't want to be uncool. And third, a cliché: you didn't ever want to be a cliché, but always extraordinary, not commonplace in any way. So I seemed together and in control, interesting and cool, up in my tower above it all, and better than anything that happened to me.

Confession: I was a needy, uncool cliché and a really lonely girl.

Our dorm suite had three bedrooms, two freshman girls in each, and a central living room, with couch, chairs, lamps and an ugly beige rug in the middle, plus a compact refrigerator and big-screen TV, courtesy of Inez's parents. After amiably agreeing about which posters would go up on the living room walls, we made another agreement: if a girl had a guy over, her roommate should sleep out on the couch. This seemed only fair and made sense, but we soon learned you had to get your combos right.

I started out sharing a room with Inez who had lived a very

cushy, protected life in the Chicago suburbs.

"I was raised in a golden cage," she told us. "Wonderful but a trap."

Now that she was liberated, Inez freaked. First weekend, first off-campus party, out on a patio that was loud, sweaty and smoky with rock music, dancing and grilling ribs, plus the sickening smell of warm beer, Inez and some other girls got up on boys' shoulders and, with other boys yelling "Flash, flash, flash!", raised their shirts and displayed their tits and not just once either, like it was an initiation, but many times. Their tits seemed to enjoy being looked at and looking back at everybody like eyes. Very liberated. Very inebriated. Welcome to college.

"If I ever do that," I said to my suitemate Wendy, who roomed with Sarah, "I'm giving you permission right now to bitch-slap me across the face."

"I'm sort of tempted, just to see what flashing feels like."

"Oh, they're all just acting like stupid college kids."

"That's what they are."

"Cliché."

College is a time for barely formed people to achieve some kind of form by trying out identities to see what works. Me, too. I was the worst and my cool mask got stuck. *Lift it off, someone, please.* But no one could. I wouldn't let them, and being off in my own atmosphere became a habit. Six weeks in college and I hadn't even kissed anyone. I was having trouble imagining a guy's tongue in my mouth; that was how bad it got.

There was a way out: drinking and taking drugs. But I didn't let myself do those things either. I thought it was uncool and disgusting to get wasted even though everyone was doing it. That's how cool and above it all I was.

Here's what would happen: at a party, people talked and shouted, people danced and drank beer, people hooked up and

left together or disappeared into bedrooms, everybody liber-
ating herself like Inez and Wendy, while I wandered among it
all like a ghost, a forbidding presence, like I was the only adult
there. In the role I was trying out for, no one was good enough
for me. They were all drunk college kids, clichés.

Rooming with Inez, I wound up sleeping on the couch a lot,
or in a chair if Sarah already had claimed the couch because
Wendy had someone over too. Once, Inez brought two guys
back from some party.

"So, one's for me right?" I cracked as I gathered my comforter
in my arms. "Thanks."

"Get your own."

Inez was escaping the golden cage at many men per hour.

Soon it became obvious that Sarah and I should share a room
because neither of us ever brought a guy home. Sharing a room
with Sarah was even more discouraging. She was a high achiever,
busy every second. She was on the swimming team and would
be on the Lacrosse team in the spring. She did volunteer work
at a shelter downtown and was going to med school though she
hadn't decided on her specialty yet. Sarah, who could survive
on very little sleep, stayed up studying all hours at her desk and
then when her alarm rang at five a.m. so she could go swim laps
and she got right up, you knew you were blessed to be in the
presence of a superior person you just had to kill.

I was a dramatic arts major, stage acting. It was a comfortable place for me to immerse myself in a character and hide. First
role I get cast in, I'm a widow whose husband has been killed by
the state for political reasons. Two men fight over me: a colonel
out of lust and a comrade of my dead husband's for other less
carnal reasons. Hovering over it all but never speaking is the
ghost of my husband who was like the gentlest guy in the world.
I've got torn loyalties. The play ends ambiguously after less than

an hour of stage time: the colonel, whose lust I share but don't act on, lifts my veil. Blackout. Half the time I had no idea what was going on. The colonel overacts, the comrade underacts, the ghost of my husband stands on risers at the back of the stage lit up from below.

No matter. It was a journey of transformation and discovery as my acting professor who was directing the play said. I immersed myself in the role. I went to thrift shops and found a black skirt and matching jacket, a black pillbox hat with a net veil and black high heels. The costume person said no to the skirt and jacket, but agreed that I could wear the hat and shoes onstage and thanked me for finding them.

Then it happened: one night, Sarah brought a guy to our room, a tall, strapping swimmer with a shaved head and shaved legs, long loose arms, big hands and a 4.0 GPA. She had met him at the pool and they trained together. The room didn't seem big enough for the athletic sex they were about to have. I gathered my comforter in my arms. That's an indelible image from that time, me gathering up my comforter from my bed and stumbling out. What was wrong with me?

"What's wrong with me?" I asked Wendy, who was in the living room.

"Guys are intimidated. You don't flirt and you don't put out any signals you're available."

"I'm not available. I'm waiting."

"Well, then, there you go: is it any wonder you don't get laid?"

"I mean, I haven't met anyone I like."

"What about the guys in the play? They seemed nice."

"One overacts, one underacts, one doesn't say anything."

"They're people, not actors. And this is life, not a play."

"Right. I should remember that."

But I didn't. Next party, the week before we opened the play, I dressed up in my widow's costume: hat, shoes, the whole bit. I spent a long time making up my face though no one could see how pretty I was unless they lifted the veil. I was gorgeous and sexy but only I knew it, waiting to be discovered, as usual. In my mind, I was a bride trapped in a widow's dress waiting for the right man to recognize me. I wanted someone so sure of himself he would lift the veil; something like that was my naïve college girl's plan.

Of course, it didn't work out. My scenario was too involved, too stupidly metaphorical and crazy and, at the end of the night, I wound up in the basement on a couch with Wendy and Josh, the actor playing the ghost of my husband. Josh needed a ride back to campus. I was the designated driver, naturally, and people still had to be gathered for the ride.

I danced with Josh a couple of times and he didn't say much, just like his ghost character in the play, but he was a relaxed dancer, as off in his own world as I was in mine and comfortable not talking, and I liked that and thought maybe all those hours being onstage with him and married to his character added up to something between us. Why not him? *Lift the veil, Josh, lift the veil*—but he didn't.

The next thing I knew I couldn't see. I must have dozed off on the basement couch and someone must have turned off the lights from the top of the stairs. My legs were stretched in front of me and my skirt hiked up to my knees from sliding down in my sleep. Hours could have passed or minutes, hard to tell, though the party had gone very quiet upstairs. I had no idea whose house it was. My eyes moved but didn't show me anything because there was no light to see by. I closed my eyes, hesitating just a few minutes more before trying to find out what was what.

I still had my widow's veil down and my black high heels on.

I was vaguely aware of the strangeness of me being in a stranger's house at who knew what hour, of the strange person I had become, half there, half in a dream, but completely isolated. Loneliness can be a drug that makes you lethargic or it can be like water you take on as you sink to the bottom. You can sink into it and there's a kind of comfort in that. You can get drunk on loneliness like other people get drunk on beer. In some strange and similar way it makes you numb to what's really happening. Did Inez know what was happening? Did I?

I felt a stirring like a whisper at the hem of my skirt where it rested against my knees. In my drowsy state, I wasn't sure it was anything or a trick of my mind. The material seemed to fold back, as if someone was doing it, weightless fingers drawing it up and away. I was a child pretending sleep and pretending not to know what was happening to her and, creepy as it sounds, I wanted to be caressed as I slept. I wanted someone so bold he would know I wanted him to do that. Crazy. My vagina felt the first sweep of blood rolling in, a surge of magnetism and heat. Of course, I couldn't let it happen. It was crazy and creepy but to stand at the brink and imagine it before anything happened was exciting.

There was still someone next to me on the couch, I didn't know who, probably Josh who had been there before. I hoped it was still him. Whoever it was took a deep breath and I took a deep breath back, a first acknowledgment, a first communication, a first agreement, maybe. Whoever it was wouldn't dare touch me without permission. But had I just given him permission with my breathing? On the staircase of seduction, each glance and word, each kiss and touch must grant permission to take the next step, but we were quiet in the dark, only breathing. I wasn't totally sure who he was but he knew me and must have thought I knew him and so in his mind it wasn't creepy at all. Unless, it wasn't Josh but some creepy stranger.

No. That made no sense, I realized later.

Through the couch, I felt the motion of his arm and of his hand sliding beneath the hem of my skirt. He hadn't touched me yet but I was going crazy, my heart beating like mad. His fingers caressed my inner thigh just above the knee, far from anywhere private, but my thighs lit up like two bright streets and every cell of my skin was aching to be touched like lips do to be kissed. I took a deep breath and he breathed back. The urge to speak was just as strong as the one not to speak. I almost couldn't take it. I don't know why I didn't speak except that I couldn't. In my mind I said, *What are you doing, Josh?* But not out loud. So I decided I was letting him.

Bolder now and with more weight and pressure, his fingers caressed me higher up, halfway there. My pussy was emanating so much heat I knew he had to feel it. He took a deep breath and I breathed back as if we were kissing, breathing through each other. I gave my hips a surrendering tilt forward and spread my legs a bit more to welcome him higher. He must know, he had to be sure I was into this with him totally now. He traced his fingers along the curve of my thigh, learning the shape of my leg and the feel of my silken skin. It's the softest, smoothest part of me, my inner thigh. Right there, I'm still a baby. I took a deep breath and he breathed back. He let the full weight of his hand rest on my thigh, very close to my cunt, which wanted to swallow his hand up but she and I waited like ladies, of course.

He turned his body toward mine, curling into me, his head above my shoulder, his mouth close to my ear, so his hand could better reach where it wanted. He breathed into my ear like a hot beast about to devour me. I breathed back. I was sopping wet and swelling with the desire to draw him inside. I tilted my hips to give him easier access and his fingers moved down through the hair of my cunt, riding over the shape of my pubic bone, to touch my hot wet flesh. He put his fingers inside me and slid them up into my vagina, which swelled to meet him and gave way, swelled and gave way. *Oh*. I made a sound, close to speech; strange to hear my own voice as I imagined he was hearing it, *Oh*. Barely disturbing the quiet.

He paused, his fingers way up inside me, and we just rested there like that as if to catch our breaths. It was so intimate and yet so strange. His hand was inside me. His breath was in my ear and we were both completely still. It felt very dreamy and, because we hadn't kissed or spoken, almost impersonal yet very human.

My hips couldn't help it: at the behest of my cunt, they started moving to make his hand move. He understood. He finger-fucked me, pulling his fingers almost all the way out and drawing his palm over my pubic bone to rub my waiting, needy clit and then plunging his fingers back in and up along the upward inner curve of my vaginal wall, long and slow and hard at the end to let me feel his strength and his intention. My flesh was hot and liquidy and, I imagined, the colors of the sunset. My flesh sucked him in and swelled around him as he drew away. My flesh waited for his hand to penetrate me again and shove into me as far up as it could go. My flesh was the ripe fruit of the gods, made for this. It wasn't going to take me long at all to come. He established a regular rhythm and I quickly learned it and tilted my hips forward and back so his hand could go all the way in and his palm could slide over my red-hot pulsing clit. My breathing got louder and quickened and he mimicked my breathing with his own, in my ear. I came screaming and bucking, my body thrown back and forth against the couch. He grabbed my pubic bone and, using it like a handle for my body, shook my entire frame in time to my shuddering. He shoved his hand way up into me and stayed there and the deeper flesh of my cunt opened to surround him. I grabbed hold of his arm to make him stop moving and stay right there, way up inside me, as I subsided. I had been a tight bud for weeks but now I had blossomed and flowered and relaxed. We settled, our breaths quieting together, staying still, his hand deep inside my cunt, normal as could be. I was warm and glowing and impersonally female and just wanted to bathe in the feeling for as long as I could before I had to be someone again.

"Wow," said Wendy, from the other side of the couch. "I guess you learned to flirt."

Wendy had been there the whole time, had probably heard it all and I didn't care. It was dark and I was crazy and relieved to be crazy and warm and dark and muddy and not cool in my tower anymore. I wasn't going to speak and ruin the quiet. I liked the craziness and the almost not knowing who it was. I still gripped Josh's arm and held it down so he wouldn't shy away now and remove his hand from inside my cunt, for just a few minutes more. It wasn't ownership and I hadn't lowered myself. It was the most natural thing in the world.

I reached down and touched Josh's erection. Even through his jeans, I could feel it pulsing, throbbing his heartbeat into my hand. I breathed my approval of his wonderful cock, a sigh, and he breathed back. His hard-on was standing straight up so the head was against his stomach and sticking out from under the waistline of his pants. I undid the button and zipped the zipper down. The release of his cock into the air, made the springs of that old couch sing. I took hold of his cock and slid my hand up and down, stroking its wonderful combination of soft silk and hard iron. I wanted to fuck him and suck him but thought, *No, not yet,* and decided in the quiet darkness of that basement a dreamy hand job with both of us staying just like we were, breathing with each other, wouldn't break the spell.

WHORE

D. L. King

The dress was red: red with a subdued intensity, a deep, wet sort of red. A red that slithered behind your eyes and rubbed up against your hypothalamus. Just seeing it on the rack caused an involuntary shiver, a contraction of my pelvic floor muscles, and made my pupils dilate. Seeing the price tag almost dissuaded me from trying it on. Almost.

It fit like it was made by my own private couturier.

The fabric was soft, with a slight nap to the hand. It draped beautifully. The dress had a high boatneck, brushing just over the top of my clavicle, but with a fitted bodice. Not too tight, just enough to enhance my small breasts and cling gently to the curve my body made from torso to waist. Long, fitted sleeves and a slight flare from the hips, ending just below my knee, completed the picture, or at least, the front of the picture. Simple and elegant.

Gazing at my reflection in the three-way mirror in the fitting room at Saks, the physical responses I had upon seeing the dress on the rack multiplied exponentially. In the back, the dress fell from the shoulder seams in a deep *V* to just above—and I do mean just above—the crack of my ass. I couldn't stop looking at the way it seemed to attach itself to my sides, following the curve in at my waist and then the beginning of the curve back out at my hips.

I turned and turned. I moved my arms and twisted my body. What made it stay glued to me the way it did? I guess you get what you pay for.

I have no idea what possessed me to bring it to the conference. What use would I have for a dress like that at a conference with a bunch of neurologists and neurosurgeons? But after three days of panels and presentations, and then finally presenting my paper, at the tail end of the last day, to a three-quarters-empty room of mostly men, checking their watches to make sure they didn't miss their airport shuttle, I'd had enough.

Knowing my presentation would be one of the last, I'd decided to take an extra night at the hotel and return home the next day, which was a good thing because I really needed a break after the last attendee thanked me for my presentation and practically ran out the door. It was only three o'clock, a little early for cocktails, so I decided to have a swim in the hotel pool and relax before dinner.

Like I said, I don't know why I brought the dress, but I do know why I put it on that night. Once rejuvenated from swimming and a nap, I realized I'd exhausted all my conference wear and I didn't think jeans and a T-shirt would cut it in the hotel's restaurant. The dress felt unbelievably sexy and I found myself being extra attentive to my makeup. I clipped my hair up in a sort of messy combination bun-ponytail, to get it off my neck. I didn't want my hair to break the expanse of bare skin from neck to ass. I remembered reading somewhere that Japanese women wore their kimonos with the neck dipping down in back because Japanese men found the back of a woman's neck sexually stimulating. Looking at the drape of the dress, I had to agree with them.

I made my way down to the hotel bar. I love beautifully appointed boutique hotels and this one, in Los Angeles, was no exception. The bar was beautifully designed in rich browns, platinum and gold and the low tables and upholstered furniture looked comfortable and inviting. A few of the tables had groups of people gathered round them, but I never felt that comfortable sitting at a table when I was alone, so I chose a seat at the bar and ordered a pomegranate martini.

The drink was perfect. I soon became lost in thoughts about one of the presentations on electrical implants and nerve pain. I raised my glass to the bartender and he nodded. As he was putting my new drink down, someone took the stool next to me.

"I've got it," a masculine voice said.

I'd guess he was about fifty, with hair graying at his temples. He wore a very expensive-looking suit and red tie. His nails were manicured. I looked from his hands to his face and he smiled.

"Thank you. Were you here for the medical conference?" He didn't look familiar, but there had been quite a few people there.

"No, I'm with the financial conference. I manage a hedge fund."

As I'd never completely understood what that was about, I asked him what he did and we spent the next half hour discussing money, finance and his life. The conversation was interesting and intelligent and, although he was older than the guys I was usually interested in, he was dead sexy. So, when he put his hand on my back and slid it down to the top of the dress and asked if I'd like to join him in his room, I didn't have to think too hard. I probably should have opted for dinner, but after two and a half martinis, my lizard brain was more interested in the meat in his pants than the meat in the restaurant.

His hand never lost contact with the small of my back as he escorted me to the elevators. His thumb continually stroked the hollow just above my ass. On the way to the thirty-fourth floor, I looked him over more closely. Maybe it was the alcohol, but I couldn't wait to see what he was hiding under those very expensive clothes.

His room was about ten floors higher than mine and had a better view. I went to the window to look out and he followed me. He bent down and kissed the back of my neck. His hands stroked my sides, over the dress before sliding inside.

"You are gorgeous," he said, hands exploring under the sides of the dress, up past the swell of my breasts and back down to my ass. He placed my hands on the window and reached down under the hem of the dress to slide it up in back. His breath caught as he ran them up my naked ass. "I don't suppose this dress is well suited to wearing panties, is it?" he asked.

I turned around and began to undo his tie and he caught my hands. "We have plenty of time for that," he said, sliding my dress up and over my head. Once off, he turned it right side out and draped it over the desk chair before taking a step back to look at me. All I had on were my shoes.

"Do you like the view?" he asked.

"Yes, I do. It's much..." His lips covered mine before I could complete the statement and his tongue parted them to explore my own. He tasted of very fine scotch, with a slight hint of expensive cigar. My hands reached up to explore his chest and he spun me around, facing the glass again.

"I like it too," he said.

Again, he placed my hands above my head and against the glass as his own stroked and kneaded my breasts before pinching and pulling at my nipples. My clit was buzzing and I could feel moisture begin seeping from my pussy as his hands stroked lower, over my ribs, down to the V of my sex. He ran his hands over the crease between my legs and my cunt.

"Spread your legs."

As I did, his hands snaked around to stroke the crack of my ass before pulling my cheeks apart. I could feel his hard cock, under his trousers, as he pressed against me. Keeping my backside open with one hand, he cupped and squeezed my pussy with the other before inserting two fingers inside my slit and spreading my lips open.

"Oh, god," I moaned as I was left open, front and rear. "Please," I murmured.

"Look at the view. I'm told you can see Catalina from here, if it's a clear day. Although I don't really know where it is. Maybe you can see it now. Are there lights on Catalina?"

I felt his thumb pressing against my anus and an involuntary shiver shook my head.

"No?"

"I don't know," I whispered. I pushed back against his hand, but he moved with me.

"Now, now. Don't get so anxious. There'll be plenty of time for that later."

I could feel my moisture coating the fingers pulling my cunt lips apart. "Please," I murmured again, rocking my hips from side to side.

"You're so wet." He closed his fingers and rubbed them against my opening. "Is this what you want? Feel how they slide." He teased my opening with the tip of one of the fingers, still keeping my lips parted with the other.

I thought I'd go crazy with desire. I'd never experienced anything quite like it before. I'm no stranger to sex; I'm a very carnal person. But this guy was directing sensations I'd never experienced before. He stopped teasing my opening and again pushed my lips apart with both fingers. He pushed the edge of his other hand deeper, splitting my buttocks even more. This time, I responded with a full body shiver.

"Lovely," he said. "Now, spread your legs farther and press your tits against the glass. Yes, that's right." He withdrew his hands and I must have made a noise because he said, "Don't worry, I'll be back. I just need to get something from the bathroom. Look for Catalina and tell me if you see it."

I fogged up the glass, panting through my open mouth. All sorts of thoughts went through my head but moving from the position he'd placed me in wasn't one of them. I saw what I was fairly certain was the Santa Monica Pier, but I still had no idea where Catalina was, or if it could be seen from here. I was just beginning to realize how inane that thought was when I felt his hand on my waist and the other rubbing between my legs.

"Did you find it?" My head shook back and forth jerkily while I felt my muscles begin to tighten pre-orgasmically. "So responsive," he whispered against my neck as he buried a finger in my pussy and stroked my clit with his thumb.

My orgasm was mind numbing in the way all little orgasms are when what you really want is a fully body release.

"Just to take the edge off a little bit," he said. He backed up and told me to turn around.

Slightly dizzy, I faced him. He was removing his tie and unbuttoning his shirt. He had a thick thatch of salt-and-pepper hair on his chest and it was easy to see that he worked out. He had a tighter chest and abdomen than the last thirty-year-old I fucked. He opened his belt and pants and removed them, along with a pair of red silk boxers, as I watched. His cock was both thick and fairly long and my mouth watered at the thought of having him inside me but first I wanted to taste him.

Silently, I knelt down in front of him and gently stroked his shaft, feeling the weight of his balls. As my lips enclosed the head of his cock I could feel all the air leave his lungs. He was warm and hard and velvety. He smelled of soap and maleness and as I tongued him, all the air left my lungs, too. I massaged his balls as I took more and more of him inside my mouth. He was too big for me to get him all the way in, so I licked and sucked up and down his shaft, paying special attention to the crown.

His hands were on my head, massaging my scalp and hair, and as I drove the tip of my tongue into the slit of his cock I could feel his balls begin to tighten. He grabbed a handful of hair and pulled my head away from his body. I strained to get his cock back into my mouth before I realized what had happened.

"Not yet," he said. "I want to come inside you, not in your mouth."

"Condoms," I whispered.

"Yes, of course. Only a figure of speech, my dear," he said. He helped me up and we walked to the bed. He pulled off the blanket and bedspread, letting them fall on the floor, and picked me up, placing me in the center of the great king-sized bed. I noticed his dopp kit on the bed table. He removed a couple of condoms and a travel-sized bottle of lube. "May I fuck your ass?"

I love anal, more I think than vaginal sex, so I smiled and said yes.

"You're sure?"

"Oh, yes," I said, drawing him to me for a kiss.

He positioned me on my hands and knees on the bed and, with one hand on my back holding me in place, he drew his other hand down my ass, gently teasing the crack. He repeated the motion several times before withdrawing his hand. "Your body is amazing," he said.

It's nice to be worshiped, and I basked in the sensation of his eyes on me until I felt cold lube dripping into my crack. His finger spread it around and began to tease me open, slowly and gently. He knew what he was doing. He was both sensuous and gentle.

"I love your ass," he said, and he inserted first one finger, then a second into me, slowly fucking me with his hand. "I can't wait to feel that tight muscle gripping me." He added more lube and kept up the gentle finger-fucking. He slipped a third finger in me and I moaned. "All right?" he asked.

"Slower, please. Just give me a minute to catch up," I panted.

He stopped fucking me and held his fingers in place. When my breathing slowed, he began his slow in-and-out motion again. I hadn't felt this full in a long time and I was eager to feel his cock in me. My clit felt heavy and swollen but I kept my hands on the bed. I wanted to wait for his cock before touching myself.

He withdrew his fingers and I felt completely empty. I whined and he said, "I think you're ready for me now." I heard him tear the condom wrapper and seconds later I felt the tip of his cock pressed against my anus and more lube drizzled over me.

He pressed slowly and steadily against me until my sphincter began to allow the entrance. He was an accomplished ass-fucker. He took his time. It was minutes before he was seated

fully inside me and I felt his balls against my vulva. I tightened my muscles against him and I felt, more than heard, him
chuckle. He hung there, without moving, letting me get fully
used to the pressure. I wanted desperately to touch myself but
I waited.

"All right?" he asked.

"Oh, yes," I sighed and he withdrew, only to slowly push
back inside. Each time he withdrew a little more and pushed
back in a little faster until I was moaning, pushing back against
him, fucking myself on his cock faster and harder.

I started to lower my head to the bed so I could take my
weight on my chest and shoulders to free my hands but he told
me not to move. He'd been keeping me steady, using my hips as
handles. He slid one of his hands around me and stroked my
cunt, only to find me dripping.

"You're one wet little slut, aren't you?" he said as he buried
two fingers inside my vagina and assumed the same rhythm he
was using to fuck my ass. "I can feel myself fucking you."

My god, my muscles were convulsing wildly around both
his cock and his fingers. I tried to get my hand on myself but he
said, no, not to do it. "You want to come?" he asked.

A low, guttural, "Yes," spewed from my throat.

"Well, you can't. Not yet."

I growled and pounded against his body, his balls slapping
against my flesh.

"I control this fuck and I'm not ready to come yet." His
rhythm changed, became more syncopated, but his fingers
stilled. He used his thumb to circle my clit without touching it
until I screamed. "Oh, the poor little slut's getting frustrated."
He withdrew his hand altogether and slapped my ass. I jumped
and my muscles tightened against him again. "Oh, yeah," he
laughed.

His rhythm built back up to a steady pounding again and he slid a finger inside me one more time. This time, instead of fucking me with it, he began to stroke the ridge just inside my opening. His strokes became harder and harder until I was panting and whining. He was still actively fucking my ass, but the pressure on my G-spot was quickly bringing me to orgasm. Before I could even say, "I'm gonna come," I was squirting fluid into his hand, something I'd never done before.

"Good girl," he said. "That's the way."

His hand slowed and withdrew but his pounding cock never faltered. After my initial tremors slowed, his rhythm picked up until it began to break up and become erratic, with more strength behind each thrust, as if he were trying to force his entire body into me, and with a few more thrusts, he came.

He grew still inside me and I felt his last few contractions as his orgasm finished. We stayed like that for a bit before he slowly withdrew to my groans of complaint. We rolled away from each other, sweating and panting, giving our heart rates a chance to slow down.

"Jesus," I said.

"You're not so bad, yourself," he laughed.

"Fuck. I never did that before. I never ejaculated before. Jesus." Once the sweat dried, I went to the bathroom to clean up. By the time I dressed and came back into the room, he'd put his pants and shirt back on. It seemed our tryst was over.

"May I have your card?" he asked. "Perhaps the next time I'm in town, I'll call you."

I was at the door. "Oh, I don't live here," I said, digging a card out of my bag. As I handed it to him, he handed me something in return. I gave him a quick kiss. "Thanks, it was fun," I said.

He closed the door behind me and as I walked to the elevator

I looked at what he'd handed me. It was money. Two five-hundred-dollar bills, to be exact. I laughed all the way down to my floor. While waiting for room service to bring my dinner I wondered what he'd thought when he read my card:

April Harriman, MD Neurosurgery
566 Park Avenue, Suite 105
New York, NY

JUST A
LITTLE TRIM

Kristina Wright

You have a new client, girl," Gil whispered in my ear. "And this boy is smokin' hot."

I dropped my bag at my station and glanced at my pink appointment sheet. "Harold Gruber? Not a hot name."

Gil looked at himself in my mirror and preened, running a comb through his jet-black pompadour. On anyone else, it would have looked dumb. On Gil, it was snazzy. I saw that he'd added a streak of white blond on one side, giving him a kind of '80s rockabilly look. I nodded in approval.

"Trust me, Lulu. Mr. Gruber is going to rock your little socks," he said, gesturing at my white anklets inside four-inch black stilettos. "And if he leaned my way, I'd be stealing him out from under you."

"Hmm." I glanced at the clock. "Well, I'm ten minutes late and Mr. Gruber is going to walk out the door if I don't get him in my chair."

I did my own once-over in the mirror. It's a hazard of being in the beauty business that I get carried away trying to look the part. I was wearing my kinky schoolgirl outfit today—sheer white blouse with a red lace bra underneath, short black skirt, fishnets, white ankle socks and black pumps. My hair—a custom mixed shade of red with a ribbon of dark purple—hung in two long braids, framing my breasts. Okay, so may be I looked more like a call girl fulfilling a businessman's afternoon fantasy instead of the top stylist at Shockwave Salon, but believe me when I say I blended in.

I walked out to the reception area, the sound of my heels clicking across the tile floor barely audible over the hum of hair dryers, and struck a pose. "Mr. Gruber?"

Whatever I had expected—and I will admit I expected a sweater vest, corduroy trousers and orthopedic shoes—Harold Gruber was decidedly not it. This six-foot-something, dark-haired, masculine beauty rose from a chair and walked toward me. The three remaining clients—two women and one college-aged skater boy, stared.

"I'm Hank," said the object of all my future wet dreams.

I licked my bottom lip, coated in a thick, glossy layer of Fuck Me Red, and smiled. "Well, Hank, I'm Lulu, your stylist today."

As he followed me to my station, I heard him mutter, "You can be my stylist any day of the week."

That gave me back my confidence and I threw a little extra sway in my sashay.

The theme of the Shockwave Salon is retro punk, with lots of black and pink and silver. The chairs are black leather and each station is a three-sided mirrored stall. Clients don't like to be stared at when they're sitting in a stylist's chair, so the reception area is separated from the salon by a wall of beveled glass. It's kind of a neat setup, really. There's an intimacy to being a stylist—it's like being a masseuse or therapist—and Norma, the owner of Shockwave, was smart to play on that.

I gestured to the chair and Mr. Gruber—Hank—settled into it. Like a bullfighter, I snapped a cape in the air before draping it around his neck. That was the first part of him I touched. His neck. I'm pretty impervious to my clients. I've only dated one and that was a disaster. I'd rather keep a client than have a date, so I lay the flirtation on hot and heavy when they're in my chair, but that's the only thing that gets laid. But rubbing my fingertips along the back of Hank's neck made me reconsider.

"So, what can I do for you today?" I said with a smile and an arch of one sculpted eyebrow.

I knew the insinuation was pure sex and that was my intention. There was a reason I was the top stylist at the salon—the only thing hotter than sex is the temptation of sex. Temptation pays the mortgage, baby.

"Just a little trim," Hank said.

I've heard the phrase before from male clients, but never said with quite the same inflection. Hank had taken my flirt and upped the ante.

"Just a little trim?" I repeated, turning my back to him.

My bag of tools was still on the floor where I had dropped it and I bent over to dig out the clippers. Thanks to the mirrors, I could see Hank's eyes go immediately to my ass. I could feel my skirt riding up precariously high. He was getting a glimpse of the stocking tops of my fishnets and maybe even a shadowy peek of asscheek, but I didn't make an effort to cover myself. The clippers were right on top of the pile, but I spent a solid minute fumbling around so he could get a good, long look. Interestingly, his eyes slipped from my bottom down to my feet before traveling back up. It looked like Mr. Gruber wasn't just an ass man; he was a leg man, too. It's good to remember such things about clients so one can dress appropriately on appointment day.

I finally stood, brushing my hand over the back of my skirt as I did. "Sorry, I'm a bit disorganized this morning," I said, a little breathless. "I had a late night and overslept this morning."

He cocked his head and studied me for a moment, as if considering what might have kept me up so late. Whatever his imagination conjured, it made him smile. "Not a problem."

I stepped behind him, meeting his gaze in the mirror. My cheeks were flushed from bending over and one braid had slipped inside my blouse. I saw him glance to where the red plait disappeared and I made a show of freeing it while giving him a better look at my cleavage. My breasts had spilled over the top of my push-up bra, so he got more of a look than I intended.

"Sorry," I said again, feeling his gaze like a touch. "How embarrassing."

I really did need to get to work on the man's hair if I was going to make up for lost time, so I focused on giving him what he wanted—just a little trim. The clippers buzzed in my hand as I trimmed up the back of his neck.

"Do you normally keep it this short?"

"This is long for me. I'm a former Marine," Hank said, staring at my cleavage as I leaned down to hear him over the noise in the salon.

"Oh. You're used to high and tight," I said, referring to the preferred military haircut. "That's practically bald."

I had moved around to the front of the chair, practically straddling his leg as I trimmed the front. My skirt had ridden up and Hank stared as I pressed my crotch against his knee. The silky fabric of the cape rubbed against my thighs and I gave his knee a little pelvic thrust. His knee never moved away. In fact, I think he might have pushed back a little bit.

"Is it?"

I was getting a little too enthusiastic about my work because I had lost track of what we were talking about. "Is it what?"

"Is it practically bald?"

I had the sneaking suspicion that Mr. Gruber was beating me at my own game. I brushed a few stray hairs from his forehead and smiled wickedly. "Oh, yeah. But some women like bald."

"Hmm. I don't think I've ever had it bald."

I moved around the chair to the other side, using the clippers around his ear. I had the overwhelming urge to lean forward and suck on his fleshy earlobe, but I figured that would be pushing my luck. Hank didn't seem averse to my flirting, but earlobe nibbling might scare him off. Or get me fired.

Even with all the flirting, I was finished with his cut in fifteen minutes. I have to admit, I was a little disappointed. I wasn't quite ready to let Mr. Gruber escape.

"That was quick," he said, sounding a tad disappointed himself.

I'm good at thinking on my feet. "Would you like a shampoo to rinse off all the loose hair?"

He looked up at me, past my breasts, an expression of dubious amusement on his face. "Isn't that a little girlie?"

"Absolutely not! It'll get all those itchy little hairs off the back of your neck."

He seemed to consider it. "Will you do it or does someone else?"

"We have a shampoo girl," I said. "But she's out sick today, so I could do it. I don't have another appointment for half an hour."

"Okay."

I unsnapped his cape and tossed it in the wicker basket by my chair. "Just follow me back to the shampoo station."

I took a few steps toward the back of the salon and realized he wasn't following me. Walking back to the chair, I started to ask why. Then I saw why. Mr. Gruber had a sizeable erection tenting his khakis. Without a word, I retrieved the cape and snapped it around his neck again.

"Problem solved. Follow me."

"Problem hidden," he said dryly. "Not solved."

We passed Gil on the way to the shampoo station. "Give me a heads-up if anyone is coming back for a shampoo."

Gil gave me a wink. "Told you, girl. Rock those socks."

The shampoo station is a dimly lit alcove with three comfortable recliner chairs and more mirrors. I got Hank settled into the chair on the end and started the water running. The salon wasn't packed today and a cursory glance at the other clients' progress told me we had a few minutes alone. I tilted Hank's head back toward the towel-lined sink and smiled.

"Relax."

He smirked, closing his eyes. "Yes, ma'am."

"Good boy," I said, running warm water over his head. "You'll enjoy this."

Having someone shampoo your hair is a sensual experience—or it can be. I was determined to make sure Hank wasn't disappointed. I lathered thick coconut shampoo in his hair, bemused by the expression of pleasure on his face. I was standing over him, my hip pressed against his muscular forearm and breasts practically in his face. He opened his eyes, staring up at me. "I can see your nipples," he whispered.

I looked down and saw that my breasts had slipped the confines of the push-up bra again. The dark ridge of each nipple was visible through my blouse.

"Oops." I winked. "I can't do much about it right now, with my hands soapy and wet. Would you help me out?"

I wasn't sure what his reaction would be, but I didn't expect him to lean up and lick one nipple through the fabric of my blouse. The sensation, fleetingly brief but electrifying, made me jump. He grinned wickedly.

"Mr. Gruber," I said, my voice all breathy. "That wasn't exactly what I meant."

"Do you mind?"

Did I mind? My salon flirtations never went beyond a little flashing and a lot of innuendo. Did I mind?

"Not in the least."

"Good," he said, before dazzling me with his ability to unfasten the buttons on my blouse with just his teeth.

"Wow. Did you learn that in the Marines?"

He chuckled. "Not exactly."

Before I could even catch my breath, Hank had two buttons undone on my blouse and was suckling one nipple. I kept lathering and rinsing his hair, at an utter loss as to what else I should do. I hoped to hell Gil had taken me seriously when I told him to warn me before anyone came back to the shampoo station.

Hank tugged at my nipple with his lips, causing me to rock forward on the balls of me feet. I was rubbing against his arm now, horny as hell and wishing I could climb on his lap and fuck him. When had this turned into *his* show? I didn't really care anymore.

"I can't do anything for you here," I said, regret in my voice, rinsing his hair until the water ran clear.

He let my nipple slip out of his mouth. "That's okay. I'm enjoying this."

I had a thought. It was insane and I wasn't thinking clearly, but glancing back toward the salon, hearing the steady buzz of the hair dryers and the hum of chatter, I was willing to risk it.

"I want to know how much you're enjoying this," I said,

thrusting my breasts in his face. "I want you to get off."

He went still against me. I expected him to pull away. It was going too far and I knew it. But I was so fucking hot I felt reckless. Hank shifted in his seat and I saw movement under the cape. He had unzipped his pants. He was stroking himself.

I moaned. The urge to rip the cape away and watch him jerk off was almost too much. But it was too risky. The whole thing was too risky and I was trying to convince myself it wasn't.

"Like that?" he murmured, nipping the swell of my breast with his teeth.

I nodded, staring at the rhythmic motion of his hand beneath the cape. "Oh, yeah," I breathed.

I gave up any pretense of washing his hair while I imagined what was going on under the silky fabric covering his lap. He sucked hard on my breast, leaving a red mark. I didn't care. I moaned, counting on the running water to drown out my voice.

"Show me," he whispered, pulling away. "I'm so fucking close."

I thought he meant my breasts, but he was staring between my legs. My skirt had ridden up as I rubbed against him, barely covering my crotch. I stood up, enjoying this moment of feminine power.

"You want to see my pussy?"

He nodded, his hand working steadily beneath the cape.

I reached down and grabbed the hem of my skirt, raising it enough for him to see. My crotch was just above eye level now and I wondered if he could smell me over the scent of coconut.

"More," he said, breathing hard. That made two of us.

I tugged my thong to the side, revealing my wet, wet pussy. "Told you it was bald," I said.

He was mesmerized, his pupils dilated and face flushed.

Hank Gruber was going to come while staring at my pussy. I couldn't resist. I dipped my middle finger between my lips, dragging moisture up over my engorged clit. I trembled, more turned on than I could ever remember being.

"Do it," he urged.

I braced my feet apart, one hand holding up the hem of my skirt, the other between my legs. I stroked myself again. One, two, three, watching Hank's hand move furiously under the cape. He was going to get off watching me get off. He was going to splatter white drops of come all over the black fabric. The mental image of what was going on just beyond my view—and my reach—was too much. I shuddered as I came, rocking back on my heels.

"Yes," Hank hissed. His eyes fluttered closed and his hips jerked upward.

I fondled my clit until I couldn't take it anymore, watching him come even though I couldn't see what he was doing.

Awareness came back to me in a rush of noise. For a few minutes it seemed like we were in our own little cocoon, but now I could hear voices—closer than I thought—and Gil talking loudly just around the wall that separated the alcove from the rest of the salon. I jerked my skirt down and tucked my breasts back in my blouse just as Gil walked around the corner. He had a look of panic on his face as he led a blond woman to the farthest shampoo chair. He shrugged apologetically at me.

"I think you're finished," I said, still sounding breathless as I turned the water off.

Hank glanced at Gil's stricken expression and laughed. "Oh, yeah, I'm finished. That was the best...shampoo...I've ever had."

Gil's client had her head in the shampoo sink and was oblivious as Hank maneuvered to get his pants fastened under the cape. He sat up and I draped a black towel around his neck to keep the water from dampening his shirt. Once he gave me the nod, I unsnapped the cape and folded it in on itself, tossing it in the laundry hamper in the corner.

"Ready to be blown?" I asked, taking great delight in watching Gil nearly swallow his tongue.

Hank stood, rubbing the towel over his damp hair. "Nah, that's okay. I don't mind it wet."

I could have sworn I heard Gil choke. His poor client was wiping water out of her eyes. "Sorry, sorry," he muttered, attempting to watch what he was doing to her but unable to take his eyes off Hank and me.

I laughed. "Well then, let's go to the reception desk and get you taken care of. You could even schedule your next appointment, if you like."

"Great," Hank said, running a finger down my cleavage. "I can't wait."

Scandalized, Gil shook his head as we left him to his poor neglected client. He called after me. "Socks, Lulu?"

I smoothed my hands down my skirt and gave him a wink over my shoulder. "Rocked, Gil. Rocked *hard*."

THREE PINK EARTHQUAKES

Thomas S. Roche

Jeff kept *staring*, but he was good-looking enough that he could get away with it. He'd stared at Molly before, from across the room, with a little less heat and a little less sleaze, though no less expectation. At the time it had creeped her out a little, but those times were long gone—what, twenty-five, thirty minutes ago? An eternity in the world of sleazy bar-pickup threesomes. Now it was almost like having a boyfriend watch her eagerly as a very hot Italian woman came in for a kiss. She was getting very throbby in places she probably shouldn't be in public, and while throbby was definitely *good*, it was also very *scary*.

Jeff looked more intently as Ilaria caressed Molly's arm. The former leaned closer, lips parted.

The latter trembled.

The latter took a deep heaving breath, and with a mingled sense of inevitability and excitement, prepared to be debauched.

As their faces neared, Molly's breath came tighter. The scent of Grapèro and brandy and clove cigarettes and the hint of a joint wafting off of Ilaria and through her slick, dark cranberry-kissable lips got Molly high all over again.

Ilaria took off Molly's glasses and slid her hand up Molly's short dress.

"I think they frown on that here," said Molly breathlessly.

"Good thing you won't be able to see them frowning," said Ilaria, her breath sweet with liquor and her Italian accent thick.

It was the kind of accent that made Molly want to put her tongue in all sorts of places.

Their lips met. Ilaria's mouth was hot and sweet. Her lips felt firm, so much firmer than the last time Molly had kissed a girl. Firmer, in fact, than the last time Molly had kissed a *guy*. Her tongue, on the other hand, was soft and wet and cool, probably from the drink. It tasted luscious. It slid deep into Molly's mouth; so distracted was she by the glorious feel of Ilaria's tongue against hers that she forgot *totally* about the hand sliding up between her thighs.

Ilaria pulled back slightly, glanced with a smirk at Molly's drink—pink and bright and untouched.

She said with purring pleasure:

"How's your Earthquake?"

"Fucking glorious," breathed Molly, and crawled under the table.

They were drinking Pink Earthquakes. As Molly would later tell all of her friends, this is not, necessarily, a good thing.

The Earthquake is a real drink. Its invention credited to Toulouse-Lautrec, the drink was the yummiest drink a girl could ask for. It was made with equal parts absinthe and cognac, about a gallon of each. It tasted like licorice, sex, death and sin.

She'd had the Earthquake before, in this very bar, Blueboy's, which had then—1995—been deep into its grand opening as "1906," or "Nineteen-O-Six" if you were saying it, rather than texting it to a fuckbuddy you wanted to meet up with.

Ninteen-O-Six had been a sort of gay bar then, if you can call anything in San Francisco a gay bar anymore. On alternate nights it was packed with hairy, howling septuagenarian Madonna queers, drag queens and Temescal-minded diesel dykes whose biological clocks were ringing so loud they practically had turkey basters in hand. Plus, of course, the twinks—who showed up every night of the week, and fucked whoever would fuck them, hungry for surrender and speed.

Nineteen-O-Six hadn't lasted. There had been seven names since then, and something like twelve re-re-openings: Trixie's, The Mint Cup, Fivey's, Tip's, The Sunbeam...and the Earthquake, introduced when it was called Nineteen-O-Six, had remained a fixture through all of those name changes.

Barely legal herself in the early days of the Earthquake—or, technically, *not* legal, but who carded in 1995?—Molly had guzzled down one-dollar Earthquakes with a terrifying zeal through happy hour and into the night, because the screaming queen bartender "Nana Puppy" (so named, in case you were wondering, because he was old enough to be a grandmother and when he wasn't tending bar he was a "lifestyle puppy") really, really liked her.

Nana P was also a history nerd, terrifying in his knowledge of just who had fucked who in 1890s San Fran. He had taught Molly all about the Earthquake, the drink, and the Earthquake, both always with a capital *E,* because as far as Nana P was concerned there was only one of each.

Of the former, the facts that had stuck in her head since Nana's departure several years ago for a Radical Puppy compound in the Appalachians were that for a brief period from

1920 to 1930, some vagabond on Powell Street made Earthquakes out of whiskey and gin and Pernod, instead of absinthe
and cognac.

Nana disparaged that "son of a bitch," believing that
"Toulouse-Lautrec had a little bit of something going on." ("I
like short men!" he'd purr as he poured and poured and poured,
mewling "Cognac! Cognac! Cognac!")

This was in the heady days of the midnineties, where worm-
wood and bisexuality were both openly decried and secretly
prized, for largely similar reasons. Bisexuality, however, was
only outlawed in the fading echoes of the women's commu-
nity. Neither bisexuality nor absinthe could be counted on, but
availing yourself of either product in San Francisco, circa 1995,
was like buying bathtub gin in Chicago, circa 1930.

She'd been twenty when she sucked down her first Earthquake, ready to drink and fuck and—well, here she was,
crawling under a table at Nineteen-O-Six to suck a hot European stranger while his girlfriend slid her thighs on either side
of her.

When, after smoking her out in the alley, they'd asked if she
played "with the couples," she'd smiled and giggled and okay,
she had to admit, even in a coquette aged thirty-six-and-change,
a tee-hee-hee-sometimes becomes a "Hell, yes" if the tee-hee-
hee goes on for long enough. And it was *really* good pot, and
Molly was single, and—Jeff and Ilaria were *hot*.

Who cared if they were leaving for Italy at 6:00 a.m.? Who
cared if they didn't even have a hotel room to go fool around
in? Who cared if she had no idea if they were really Italian, or
serial killers, or both.

They were fucking *hot*.

The special of the night was Pink Earthquakes—the same
drink as the Earthquake introduced by Nana Puppy, but with

added Grapèro, a pink grapefruit liqueur. It made no fucking sense, because the word *Grapèro* looked and sounded like grape. But it was indeed pink, and mixed with cognac and absinthe it indeed shook the world.

And how they'd ended up with three of them on the table (their second round) was almost—*almost!*—as shaky. After he'd smoked her out in the alley and his girlfriend had propositioned her for a threesome, Chiaffredo—or Jeff, as he told me to call him—had said, "What you drink, we drink!"

And that was the provenance of the three Pink Earthquakes that sat half consumed on the table, working their magic on Molly—which is how she ended up under the table, her face in Jeff's crotch and Ilaria coiled around behind her, thighs on either side, holding Molly's long wispy hair out of the way so she could lean down and watch.

Molly fumbled a bit with Jeff's belt, which was a skinny, smooth, Italian job, slippery with not much to grab on to. You would have thought she'd given Ilaria the greatest gift in the world; the wiry little brunette slid half under the table so she could moan rapturously at Molly, "Let me help," then got her boyfriend's belt and button open like she had done it a million times—maybe two million—in sleazy gay bars while tarty little thirty-six-year-olds drooled over what was beyond.

Molly handled the zipper, though—that was her singular pleasure. It came down easy, unlike the belt, and the smooth silky drape of his pants felt good on her face as she kissed his cock through the stretched, smooth fabric. *Are those panties?* Molly wondered as she slid her tongue along the length of Jeff's dick. But no, they weren't panties—just some kind of spacey, ultrastylish, Italian banana hammock that made Jeff, for some inexplicable reason, seem that much more Italian to her, and that much more erotic. She eased the springy fabric down and found it eminently practical—it tucked beneath his balls with frightening ease, and stayed there as Molly took a breath and pressed her mouth to the smooth, soft-hard surface of Jeff's cock. Having gotten lots of practice at giving head in recent years with Carl—the ex who was thankfully no longer spoken of—Molly was surprised to discover she'd missed it. Of course, she hadn't missed sucking a stranger's cock under a table in Blueboy's—because that, she'd never done before. The combination of familiar cock in her mouth—technically unfamiliar, sure, but seductively comforting—and the filthy knowledge that she was doing something she shouldn't made her so fucking horny her head started to spin. Recognizing this heady sensation, she pushed through it and made love to Jeff's cock with dangerous gusto. She drooled just enough to make things easy as she curled her fingers around his weighty girth; then she slid her mouth down, feeling lipstick-sticky-bitter mingling with sticky-Grapèro-sweet. She was already wet, already as thoroughly pulsing with sexual energy as she had ever been in her life, as she took her sticky lips down to the halfway point of Jeff's cock and began to make love to it with her tongue, bobbing and slurping and drawing great deep breaths of cologne-free sweat with undertones of weed and sex and soap. To her, that was hot—very hot.

With pleasure she mused that Jeff knew enough to not wear cologne on his balls—unlike the other Italian guy she'd slept with, in a European hostel fifteen—sixteen?—years ago. He also knew to shower before he came to a bar with his unbelievably hot girlfriend to pick up slutty American girls—just long enough ago to give his dick that intoxicating taste of *cock*, but give the rest of him the irresistible faint scent of fresh-scrubbed guy.

And he had been a perfect gentleman so far.

He'd even let his girlfriend be the one to proposition Molly, and not until *after* they'd smoked her out. He hadn't even leered at her, really, not like a sleazebag, at least, until after he got the go-ahead from his girlfriend. See? Perfect gentleman.

When Molly was in certain moods—like this one—sometimes that was all it took to make her seriously want a guy.

So she was already wet to the knees when she slid her mouth down on his cock and felt it nudging the roof of her mouth. She wanted him majorly—wanted to fuck him, even. Maybe she'd go back to their hotel room and spend the night—fuck, that would be *dirty*. More dirty or less dirty? Just dirty. Dirty enough. Dirty enough for a thirty-six-year-old. Dirty enough for a fag, not to put too fine a point on it. Dirty enough for a total drooling slut.

She was already wet to the knees, enough to feel her fucked-open cunt, still aching from Ilaria's fingers, dripping out around her cockeyed panty-crotch. Molly felt the icky scrape of the edge of her underwear against the sensitive bit between her lip and her thigh, and it felt sticky, wet and drippy. Ilaria, clearly expert in the fingering of women, left something to be desired in putting their panties back in place when she was done.

But then, as it turned out, she wasn't done.

Molly felt Ilaria's hands going into her dress. Molly was deep in the dark, now, the strobe lights from the dance floor nothing more than flashes through her eyelids. But she could feel everything that was going on all around her. Ilaria's thighs came close around Molly's hips and did something midway between pinning her in place and caressing her. Molly felt at once controlled and taken care of. *Hot*, she thought. *Fucking hot.*

The spindly Italian girl leaned down tight under the table and put one hand up Molly's dress, plucking her soaked-through panties out of the way and easily sliding into her—three fingers, knuckles deep, pads of the fingers on her G-spot. Without even knowing she was doing it, Molly rocked back and forth, feeling icky-sticky Blueboy floor on her knees and not even caring. She worked her hips and fucked herself doggy-style onto Ilaria's fingers, seeing stars when the Italian woman's thumb found her clit and gently, then more firmly, caressed it.

Molly kept sucking Jeff's cock, having moderate trouble concentrating until she just let her habits with Carl take over. Then, at least toward the end, she hadn't really liked it that much—it had been an obligation, made more bothersome by the fact that she had formerly liked it so much. But now she *loved* it. She'd forgotten how much fun it could be to give head.

Ilaria took a break from fingering Molly to pull her panties down her thighs. Molly tried to put her legs together, but Ilaria wasn't having it; she splayed her cunt-wet fingers and pushed them back open. Molly felt the stretch of her panties at her knees. It reminded her what she was doing. It reminded her that her panties were down; it reminded her she could not easily take them off. She was under a table at Blueboy's, her panties around her knees. It felt like a fucking dog collar: basically, in a good way. In a *really* good way.

Having pulled Molly's panties down, Ilaria's hand went back between her thighs—but not to finger. She started spanking her. Not Molly's ass—that would have been hot, but not quite crazy-hot. Not quite insane with fucking hotness. No—Ilaria spanked Molly's cunt, smooth and hard, none of this warm-up shit and none of this asking if she liked it. She just spanked, and when Molly trembled and pumped her hips madly, Ilaria spanked harder and faster, the smacking sounds unmistakable under the pulse of dance music—but for once in her life, Molly didn't give a damn if people heard.

Molly was close, fast—so close she barely knew it was happening; all she knew was that something had started to go very wrong, or right, or different, inside her. What was this fast swirling churn of her stomach? What was this twitch in her hips, this weakness in her thighs?

A fucking orgasm.

Ilaria seemed to gauge the moment exactly. She pulled back from the spanking and started fingering Molly again, two fingers in and up against her G-spot, thumb on her clit. It was so hot Molly didn't think she could stop herself. It was going to happen. She sucked and rocked and fucked herself onto Ilaria's hand and moaned around Jeff's dick and sank into the sensations, knowing she was utterly out of control, now.

She wondered: *How is it that I'm thirty-six years old and just now doing this?*

Then Ilaria's thumb found some special angle on her clit, and her fingers found her G-spot again and Molly didn't think much of anything.

Instead, she fucked herself back and forth, because she realized with eager guilt that she was going to climax.

Ilaria knew it, too; whether Jeff got the memo Molly would never know or care. She never stopped sucking him, exactly, but he must have known; she went from smooth, hot, dripping-wet rhythmic strokes of mouth-on-dick to lips on balls and a shuddering, all-over breakdown, her breath coming choppy and dangerous against his gloriously delicious crotch.

She came explosively, pussy clenching and trembling around Ilaria's fingers.

Molly wasn't even done climaxing before she started sucking cock again. She realized with eager surrender that she wanted to swallow his come—a bad idea, maybe, not entirely safe, and of course she'd never do it—unless, of course, he just sort of squirted without warning, and in that case, well...she'd have to. And she'd like it. Otherwise, she'd pull away at the very last minute, and he'd need a trip to the bathroom. She wouldn't swallow, but she wanted to, and after too long with Carl giving half-asleep blow jobs, Molly realized just how *fucking awesome* it was to want something dirty like this. Sucking cock under a table in a gay bar was one thing. Eating come was quite another, super-filthy and hot as hell.

Molly had long ago gotten out of the habit of doing that. Her youthful obsession with Matt and Steve and then Roger had made it hot as hell to take "them" into her body. But since then—ten years, now—she'd gotten in the habit of being a finish-with-a-hand-job girl, occasionally a facial, because men always seemed to love that so much (which always made her think *huh?*) but far more often a tit shot because, have you ever tried to get come out of your hair? It requires a cold shower. Tits were far more easily lathered and rinsed, or just wiped off if you were late for work.

But here she was, single again and thirty-six and wanting to swallow a stranger's come under the table at Blueboy's—still tasting Pink Earthquakes as she swirled her tongue and worked her mouth eagerly all over his dick. Here she was, turned on enough to swallow, and she *craved* it. But she knew she couldn't have it, for safety's sake, and that was almost as delicious as knowing she could.

Then she thought:

Holy shit, I want to fuck this guy.

Not at home, not in some dumb hotel room—right here, under the table, in the bar.

Of course, she knew that, like swallowing his come, such a desire was ridiculous. It was crazy. She couldn't do that. It was ridiculous to even want such a thing.

Wasn't it?

* * *

Blueboy's, like 1906 and all the other bars before it, was a magic place. Things *happened* there.

Giving head was something she could get away with. With the crowd packed like this, no one could see a damn thing. The bouncer would never bounce them, and despite its size it could be a tight, savvy crowd here at Blueboy's. It was a gay crowd. She'd seen it a thousand times before, sometimes in this very booth. Every guy who hung out here seemed to know it. If you noticed someone giving head under a table, you backed in and dragged your friends in there to give him room to work without getting nabbed by the bouncer—who, to be sure, didn't care, but knew the health department would.

But letting him fuck her would be going too far, wouldn't it? These Italian people didn't have to come back here next week. She'd been coming here for fifteen, sixteen years. She *had* to come back here. She couldn't just...*fuck* here, under a table.

Or could she?

As she drove Molly to greater heights of hunger, Ilaria's other hand reached up and—probably because she could not get purchase if she reached above Molly's shoulder, Ilaria tucked her hand through the loose sleeve of Molly's dress— slid up smoothly under her lacy, laundry-soft, too-old, too-well-worn bra.

Her hand felt warm on Molly's tits; the air conditioner had started to blow, and she was right in the vent. Her goose bumps made her crave the warmth not only of Ilaria's hands on her, but of Jeff's crotch all over her face. He caressed her hair and gently stroked her face. It was weird not to be able to see him, but he was leaning forward.

Ilaria's fingers worked her nipples. She pinched and stroked, gently digging her nails in, tentatively at first—and then more firmly.

Molly moaned around Jeff's cock, opened wide and slid down till her lips were around his cock's base. She hadn't done that in forever—deep-throating, something she used to totally like. Or had she just liked it because Carl liked it? *Academic, purely,* she decided. She liked it *now.* She liked it because not only did she have a hot Italian stranger's cock down her throat; she had his girlfriend pinching her nipples while she finger-fucked her deep and thumbed her clit. Goddamn, she was fucking hot.

She wanted to fuck.

She really, really, *really* wanted to fuck. If she'd been anywhere other than here, she would have done it, without question. She almost wanted to do it here. Well...maybe not just almost.

Molly realized that was, of course, ridiculous. She didn't have a condom. She wasn't on the pill. Not to imply, for an instant, if she *was* on the pill, she would have fucked an Italian stranger in a bar without a condom. That would be bad. She wouldn't do it. She was about 98 percent sure. No—99 percent. 95. Maybe 90. That 2 or 1 or 5 or 10 percent made her feel so drunk and crazed and horny and very scared for a second, until she felt the creaking of the table above her and felt a stab of panic that banished her sense of *I'm about to do something bad.*

Jeff and Ilaria were kissing.

Fuck, that was romantic. Molly's heart swelled nigh to bursting. She wasn't having sex with some weird Italian swingers; she was exploring her sexuality with a couple that totally loved each other. She was making love to love itself, right?

On her knees. On a sticky bar floor. Half drunk on sickly sweet Pink Earthquakes and—okay, she was a fucktoy. A sleazy little kneeling fucktoy. Was that bad?

She slid her mouth off Jeff's cock, panting and drooling,

realizing her makeup was ruined and her eyes had been running. She must look a total mess, she decided. *Hot*.

The table creaked some more, and Ilaria slid down half under the table—a feat that would have been completely impossible in the tight confines of the bench, if she hadn't been one of those Italian bitches who apparently crave nothing but salad and cigarettes.

Well...almost nothing.

Ilaria's hands plucked Jeff's cock out of Molly's mouth—like a nanny taking away a naughty girl's toy. Molly began to think she'd gone too far—was this jealousy? She'd read the guidebooks. Jealousy was guaranteed in any threesome, even with Italian strangers.

Then Ilaria leaned down deep under the table. They couldn't have kissed, crammed under the table like that—but Molly wanted to.

Ilaria's mouth was wet and warm against Molly's ear.

"Do you eat my pussy?" she asked.

Molly breathed hard.

"What about him?" she asked. Her voice was hoarse. Her throat was thick from cock and lust.

Ilaria said, "Let him fuck you as you do."

Molly felt a hot wave of excitement.

Was she really going to do this?

She said, "Do you have—"

The condom was already in Ilaria's hand. She tore its package delicately. It wasn't some shady Italian brand; it was a Kimono. An instant later, Ilaria had it out of the package and rolling down easy over her boyfriend's cock.

That answered Molly's question.

Yes, she was really going to do this.

Ilaria helped Molly turn around, her knees sticking dirty

and icky to the floor. As she did, Molly slipped one foot, then
the other, out of her panties and felt Jeff's hand close around
her—plucking them out of her hand. He spirited them away.
What was he going to do with them? Huff them? Here at Blueboy's, guys would just think he was huffing Amyl. That was
kind of vaguely hot.

Molly spread her legs, her knees tucked between the post of
the table and the floor. She spread her knees wide and put her
ass in the air. She felt Jeff's hand teasing her smooth, hairless
pussy lips open with his thumb and forefinger; two other fingers
curled lazily in the strip of her pubic hair as Ilaria opened her
thighs and guided Molly's face between them. Ilaria's short
dress rode up. She didn't wear underwear. Ilaria wasn't trimmed
like Molly—she was fully, beautifully natural. The scent of her
pussy was intense, a hot-wet musk smell mingled with cigarettes
and liquor.

How long had it been since Molly had gone down on a
woman?

A while. A decade? Half a decade, maybe—there was that
lackluster threesome with that girl Carl dated during their poly-
amory phase. What was her name? Katrina? Karen? Kara?

It was, she discovered, like riding a bike.

Right there under the table at Blueboy's, Molly felt the first
man since Carl *entering* her as she pressed her mouth to his
girlfriend's juicy sex. His cock was thick at the head—just thick
enough to stretch her a little, *exactly* at the place where *a little*
met *enough* met *a lot* met *more than enough* met *almost exactly
too fucking much*—and that meant almost. Exactly. Too much.
But not quite, which was just fucking right.

Ilaria was *perfect*—wet as a faucet inside but dry enough
outside that it took a long slow wriggle of Molly's tongue to

find the moisture. Then there was the taste, overwhelming her—deeply intoxicating, sexy and bewitching. Then there was the smell, all around her, drowning out everything else. Horny pussy. *Why the hell did I ever stop sleeping with girls again?*

Oh, thought Molly. *That's right. True love, or something. Fuck that. Never again.*

Once his cockhead had breached her entrance, Jeff paused, gently working into her, like he worried his massive throbbing enormity might hurt her. She wondered: *Nice Italian Boy, or Pompous Stud With Delusions of Grandeur?* He went much too slow for her taste, as if to make sure he didn't hurt her. *He won't hurt me*, she decided, but what a perfect gentleman. She fucked herself onto his cock while sliding her tongue deep between Ilaria's lips, teasing clit and pussy and sliding two fingers up inside her. Along with her apparently 10 percent body weight (all of which was in her tits), Ilaria apparently had an appetite not just for salad and cigarettes, but for one-finger-at-a-time, to judge how it felt when Molly slid three into her. She was snug—so very snug—and as Molly started fingering her, she felt the total absence of Ilaria's G-spot—was this some sort of a trick? Did only Irish girls have them, or something?

Jeff might have had delusions of grandeur, but his cock was indeed sufficiently sized so that Molly felt the head against her cervix as she fucked herself onto him. He really couldn't do much without giving the game away—after all, anyone who looked at the table and saw him pumping away underneath would have—well, would have thought it was just another night at Blueboy's. But that anyone would have expected her to be not a thirty-six-year-old slut but a whorish twink who hitchhiked here from Tuskegee with a fake ID and an attitude. She had the attitude, at least. She squeezed her muscles tight around Jeff's cock and gauged the rhythm, feeling him struggle to stay still so she could do the work it took to get him off—down under the table, on her knees, ass in the air, pumping a stranger's hard cock off inside her. Simple as giving a hand job, which she'd done—but a thousand miles beyond it on the Sleaze Scale.

Some guys are easier than others—Jeff was complicated. It took concentration to push him over—so her mouth on Ilaria's clit was not doing its job. The poor Italian girl seemed thoroughly pleased nonetheless—as, with her thighs closed around Molly's pumping body, she leaned over, hard against the table, as did Jeff.

What Molly finally settled on to finish him off—and it turned out this worked perfectly—was to squeeze her muscles *hard*, in the exact rhythm she'd always used to get Carl off. It felt so sleazy to do—but what do you know?

The couple kissed deeper and felt each other up far above her—their passion making the table tremble.

Molly felt the rhythmic pattern of their kiss as Jeff's hips jerked, and a faint swelling—almost undetectable—told her something was happening down there. He was coming in her— or, to be more accurate, in the condom, which was both yummy and comforting.

Then the table started to shake, and creak, and moan as if about to collapse atop Molly, as Jeff grabbed the edge of it and Ilaria fought to steady him. The whole table shuddered as if in an earthquake—and Molly didn't stop. She just squeezed her pussy muscles harder and milked his dick until he stopped.

Before she knew what was happening, Molly felt Ilaria pulling her up to the bench alongside her. She came up red faced and gasping, her mouth wet and makeup ruined. Jeff worked the condom off him and wrapped it in five cocktail napkins— had he stacked them there in advance, in anticipation of this moment? Regardless, he still had her panties. He grabbed them and stuffed them in her pocket.

Ilaria pulled Molly's dress down quickly—in response to Molly's querying eyes, she jerked her head toward the door.

The bouncer was fighting through the crowd toward them, looking pissed.

No way. Someone had narced on them? At *Blueboy's*?

Times just weren't what they used to be.

Molly put her mouth to Ilaria's ear and said, "I didn't get to make you come."

Ilaria glanced at her slim silver watch—almost last call.

Ilaira said, "It is long to the airport? Cab? I don't remember. I was so horny when I came. Is it a long cab ride?"

Molly opened her mouth to say *Not really, at this hour,* but thought better of it.

She smelled Ilaria's cunt on her fingers and purred, "Long enough for an Earthquake...."

BELLE DE SOIR

Austin Stevens

She is not the kind of girl who turns heads, really. But she's turning them now, which is good enough for her.

Men stare as Steffi strides through the lobby of the Damiano, past the spendy restaurant and the trendy boutiques. Perched on very high heels and poured into a *very* small dress—curvy and tight—she walks past men who practically drop their jaws as they stare at her, trying not to *look* like they're staring.

She sees them. She likes them. She likes them, as a group, to be reduced to grunting apes. She thinks she might just get her rent paid after all.

Her name is Stefanie Murray and she's twenty-three years old. She's not a tall woman when she's not wearing five-inch spike-heel pumps. They're red, like her dress. There's more to the shoes; there's practically nothing to the dress. It plunges between her tits, it stretches at her thighs as she walks. It hikes in the back just enough that the hem reveals the tops of her sheer black stockings. They have seams down the back and garters at the top. She has a tasteful pattern of flower tattoos traced up each calf to her knee, which gives men's eyes an excuse to go down and then up and then down again.

In the eyes of the men who stare hungrily at her in the lobby of the Damiano, that skintight red dress stays attached to her flesh against all laws of physics; with each sway of her hips, each jiggle of her tits, each toss of her hair and each lift and stretch of her arms or her shoulders or splitting of her thighs as she walks, the painted-on garment threatens to peel away off of cleavage and crack and round cheeks and ripe thighs and whatever dirty filthy things a girl like this might be wearing under a dress like this. If anything at all.

A dress like this on a woman like Stef makes men, mostly older men, extremely dull and stupid; that's how she likes them. Dull and stupid and handing her six hundred dollars.

It feels good to have the men looking at her, even if she can't really see them. Steffi's not very good at this—or at least, she's not experienced. This is her very first time, and as the agency said: "Impress him. You might get a repeat."

Steffi doesn't want a repeat, but she wants six hundred dollars. Or, more accurately, three-forty after the agency's cut.

And Steffi wants men to look at her, starting with the men in the lobby—or, rather, the parking valet before them, and the three men in the elevator who couldn't take their eyes off of her.

She's not really sure which is more important: the sex or the money.

The money, surely. But who says she can't enjoy herself?

Wear something classy, Steffi Murray had been told by Jeanette, the owner of Private Lives Personal Consultants—the madam, if you must—when she called to book her first assignment. Jeanette had said, *Wear something classy, and sexy but subtle, or the concierge will know what you're there for. Sure, you might get away with it today, and tomorrow, but they'll know what you're doing and sooner or later you'll get kicked out. It's bad for business. Guys don't want a whore; they want a girlfriend. And concierges really don't want a whore walking through their lobby with everyone knowing what she's there for. If you want to stay in this job and if you want to get regulars, you'll play it sexy but subtle, Sessa.* Subtle.

But "Sessa" doesn't *want* to stay in this job. She doesn't want any regulars. What she wants is a thousand bucks, made in a day, or maybe a day and a night and, if she has to, a nooner. Today and tomorrow—that's all.

She's had fantasies her whole life about getting paid for sex. She's been bewitched by the thought since her early days, obsessed with *Pretty Woman, Belle de Jour,* Victorian porn. Now she gets to be one—but just until tomorrow.

Today is Friday and she wants Saturday to pack and she has to be on a plane at 6:00 a.m. Sunday. And more importantly, she wants this all to be fast so she doesn't have too much time to think about it—because she wants it very, very much, but isn't stoked about admitting it to herself.

That's why, as she walks through the lobby, she's wet. That's why, as men leer at her, she's very, very wet. That's why she's horny—very horny. Fucking *dying* of need, having thought about her first trick all morning, ever since Jeanette called at 8:00 a.m. to offer it. Sessa's nipples peak firmly enough to show through the fabric. Her sex feels smooth beneath her dress, freshly shaved and dripping, exquisitely sensitive.

She takes the elevator with more suit-clad businessmen who can't take their eyes off her; she wishes she could see them better. But her horn-rimmed librarian glasses sit perched on the dash of her '86 Civic; they don't go with the ensemble.

And contacts?

Steffi can't even put eyedrops in.

Itchy pieces of plastic are out of the question.

Sure, "Sessa" could handle it, but "Sessa" is a fantasy—an illusion. For Steffi, with her wet shaved puss and her shelf ass and aching nips, as much as for the guy about—she hopes—to fork over six hundred dollars for sex.

She looks the businessmen up and down salaciously, pursing her red-painted lips.

She can't see them that well; they're quite blurry. But she smells them, cologne and male sweat wafting along with her and mingling with her whore-perfume as she stalks in mincing steps down the hall—to Room 2332.

She checks her cell phone: it's 3:59. Right on time.

She takes a deep breath, licks her lips; thinks, *Okay. Don't get scared. It's just sex, right? It's just fucking. No big deal.*

Yeah, just fucking for money, she thinks, and her insides give a hot scary quiver.

She knocks thrice: hard, deep and even.

The door opens. A man in his thirties answers; Steffi feels a sudden rush. This guy's *hot*. Psyched up as she is to fuck a stranger—a revolting, repulsive stranger if it comes to that, and she won't care all that much if it does—she isn't going to have to. In fact, she's pretty okay doing this guy. He's fucking *handsome*. He's wearing a suit with suspenders—fucking *hot*. Gordon Gecko shit. He's much closer, physically, than the guys who lusted after her in the lobby, so he's not just a blur. Even Steffi's 20/100 tells her he's got a fuckload of *Mrrrrowr!* going on.

She tinkles out musical notes, fake-soprano: "Hi, I'm Sessa. Are you Jason?"

He throws his tongue around his mouth a few times, like it's

just been shot full of Novocain. Steffi feels a hot wave of pleasure go through her; holy shit, she's made him a mute. This guy
is hot, and she made him stupid. Add six hundred dollars and
Romeo's her dream date.

He finally says, his eyes wide and zinging in circles all around
her and over her—everywhere but her tits and her legs—"Yes,
I'm Jason. You're Sessa?"

"That's what I said," she purrs smoothly. "Can I come in?"

He gets red and embarrassed; he backs up and holds the
door and lets her in. He can't stop looking at her, but he can't
let himself look at her. She guesses the dress is a hit.

Her cell phone buzzes. She ignores it.

She looks Jason up and down and says, "You seem nervous.
Can I help? It's really nice to meet you."

He laughs nervously. "I didn't expect you to be so hot."

Steffi feels a warm glow. The dress is *definitely* a big hit.

So she drops it, smooth and even—practiced thirty times
in her bedroom. It goes down so easy—just a *snap*, and a *zip*,
and a *wriggle*—Jason barely even knows what she's doing, until
the dress is a puddle of cherry-red blood on the floor around
her spiked heels. She steps out of it and with the toe of one
cherry-red shoe, she tosses the dress onto a nearby chair with
her handbag. She smiles.

"I didn't expect *you* to be so hot," she says. "You know it's
okay to look, don't you?"

So he does, panting, wanting her, his eyes drinking in the way
her tits spill out of her tight push-up bra, the way her hips roll
from under the soft lace of her garter belt and her thighs spread
her garters. Her shaved sex is visible, beautifully so, through her
nearly transparent thong with barely anything to it.

She said, "I'm afraid I have to ask you—"

Jason points at the bedside table; there are eight crisp

hundreds there, spread out in a fan. Steffi feels a rush.

"Just let me take care of this," she says, and Jason nods. She walks over to the bedside table and makes a very big show of bending down so he can get a good look at her ass. She feels the cool hotel air on her sex—she's wet, very wet; is this really as hot as she's making it?

Fuck no, she decides—it's *hotter.* Even if the sex turns out to be bad, she's going to fantasize about this moment for the rest of her fucking life.

She tucks the money in her bra and minces past him to the chair that holds her handbag. She puts the money in her wallet, palms a condom and returns to him. She edges up to Jason, putting her arms around him and her body up against him.

She sighs: "Wanna take me to bed?"

He does.

The sex isn't bad. He isn't the genius sex-god of the universe, but as turned on as Steffi is, he doesn't need to be. She helps him out of his clothes and pulls the covers back and spreads him out on the bed and takes his cock in her mouth. She sucks his dick with an eager abandon; *I'm getting paid for this,* she thinks. *I'm getting fucking paid for this.* She's never been the sort of girl who has an easy time being present in the moment during sex, but now it's ten times harder to be so. Not because he's a stranger; not because he's a client. Because all she can think is, *Two-sixty from eight is five hundred and forty. Five hundred and forty fucking dollars. Five hundred and forty! And he gave me a two-hundred-dollar tip before I'd done anything. Holy shit!* She can't fucking handle it. She thinks *Venice*; she thinks *Rome*; she thinks *Job applications in the fall*; that makes her freak so she goes nuts on his dick and starts laying down the porn-star action that's always been guaranteed to make whatever guy she's with think she's some kind of sex goddess. Except Jason already does.

He pulls her off of him, gasping and glancing at the clock.

"Don't make me come," he pants. "Fuck, you're good at that! Here, let me—"

He rolls her over on her back and slides her thong down. She learned a slutty trick from a porn novel about a prostitute: when wearing a garter belt, your underwear goes on the outside. Jason takes the thong off of her over her red high heels and tosses it on the bed as he goes down on her. He's good at that—*very* good. Very *very* fucking good. Maybe she's just turned on enough that it doesn't really matter if he's good. Or maybe he's *great*—the best clit-licker in the business. Either way, she's clawing crisp hotel sheets up and biting pillows soon, moaning, thighs doing things they shouldn't, begging him not to stop.

He doesn't. She boxes her ears. Her back arches. She yells. Her ass goes up and fucks his face. He rides her carefully. He does something with his mouth and some kind of suction and the way his tongue moves is *nice*. She comes fucking *hard*. She collapses moist with sweat, a puddle of moisture underneath her. She grabs the condom from the nightstand, tears off her bra and pulls Jason onto her.

She gets the condom on *fast* and then he's inside her—*voila*. Two minutes, three at the outside. He tries to last; after all, she's really moaning. She seems to be enjoying it lots; he wants to make it last.

And she *is* enjoying it—but she can hear her cell phone buzzing, over in her purse tucked against her wad of hundreds. She wants that even more than she wants Jason's very hot dick, and as good as it feels inside her, it's the feel of his tongue and the explosion of her orgasm, so beautiful and so unexpected, that Steffi will recall with pleasure and pride like a pair of gorgeous events in the timeline of her life.

Jason lets go and sighs and comes inside her—in the condom. She helps him off her, removes and ties the condom off, and cuddles with him briefly. Then as he rests, panting, she's off to check her phone, kicking off her shoes and unhitching her garter belt as she does.

She says, "You mind if I take a shower?"

"Not at all," he says.

She texts Jeanette back: *NP, will c client @ Griffin on 1st St @ 6. Rm #?*

Jason watches her cross the room to the bathroom. When she gets out of the shower, he's gone—and there's another hundred-dollar bill on the pillow, smelling like her perfume.

She puts her clothes on.

She feels bad about lying to Jeanette. *Yes, I'm looking to make a career of this. I'm in it for the long-term. It's not just a lark. Oh, I'm very sexually free. I want to learn from you and the other girls. I want to learn the business.* It was all bullshit; what she wants is money, and fast, enough so she won't have to call her parents and beg halfway through the post-graduation European trip they opposed with vehement savagery. "You should get a job," her father told her.

Steffi guesses she has. This is definitely a job. Otherwise, how'd she get five hundred dollars?

She was enjoying herself, but that just makes it a *good* job.

And it's a temp job, she guesses—just for a day and night.

And maybe a nooner, if she has to.

If she *has* to.

Dressed again and primped and perfumed, she takes a taxi, because she doesn't want to fuck around with her glasses or with finding parking. She disembarks at the Griffin, where the second client waits in Room 1254.

He's in his early fifties; his name is Dennis and he's reasonably hot and suave and sexy. She feels dirty for doing a man as old as her father. She kind of likes that.

Dennis doesn't tip her up front, but he goes down on her, too, and what he lacks for in shaving technique he makes up for with a tongue that's clearly seen a lot of women. Drunk and cocky for having done it once for Jason, she looks down at Dennis's handsome face with his mouth eagerly working on her clit—and tells him he should keep doing that a little, if he wants her to come for him.

He does and she does, but it's harder the second time. What she does, finally, after ten or twelve minutes of trying and not quite getting there, is caress Dennis's face and ease his mouth off her clit—then slide her finger down and rub herself fervently; that part she's good at. She comes *hard*, and he's got the condom on before she even sucks him. He enters her gently, sighing, "Is that all right?" He's got a somewhat biggish cock so he must be used to women complaining. Steffi doesn't complain; she says it's way fucking more than all right, and it is. She wraps her legs around him and kisses him deeply as he fucks her; Dennis seems shocked at that.

Oh, right, thinks Steffi. *Prostitutes don't kiss, I guess.*

Then she thinks, *Holy crap—is that what I am?*

The thought turns her on so much she can't help herself. She rolls Dennis onto his back and rides him slowly looking into his eyes and sliding her hand down her front and panting, "You mind if I come again?"

That shocks him even more than the kiss, but of course he says go right ahead. She rubs eagerly, looking down at him as she masturbates while riding his dick. She never realized her thighs were this strong. She's been working the stair-stepper all year—not the better to fuck, but the better to hike the fucking Alps—and now it's paid off. She fucks herself on him, rubbing with one hand, caressing his chest, using every dirty word she can think of as she tells him how good it feels.

It takes her ten minutes; when her climax comes, it's intense but achy, like she's pushed her body too far. She slumps forward and rides him and begs him to come.

He flips her over and fucks her; he comes in a minute. She kisses him, smiles, says, "Thank you."

"No, no, thank *you*," is Dennis's shocked response—along with another two hundred.

Steffi doesn't shower this time; she just tucks the money in her bra, because she really really *really* likes to feel it there.

As she takes a cab back to the Damiano to retrieve her car and her glasses, her cell phone buzzes.

It's a text from Jeanette.

WTF is up with you???

Steffi texts back: *???*

Jeanette: *Jason just emailed to brag he got you off. Guess u enjoyed? LOL.*

Steffi: *LOL.*

Jeanette: *He wants 2 c u next week.*

Steffi: *Sorry, out of town.*

Jeanette: *:-(You said early 2morrow was good?*

Steffi: *Til midafternoon.*

Jeanette: *How bout 12 and 2? Both at the Dami?*

Steffi: *2 clients?*

Jeanette: *Yah 2 today, 2 tomorrow - kewl?*

Steffi takes a deep breath. She feels a rush of excitement as she thumbs back:

OK KEWL.

Feeling warm and glowy all over, Steffi gives the driver a tip and crosses the lobby to the parking elevator on the far side, even though she doesn't really have to. She just likes walking through the lobby. Men in the growing Friday crowd watch her every move with gusto. Venice will *rock* this year.

And she's gonna have that nooner after all.

THE SPOILED BRAT

Lily K. Cho

Amy paused to check the name on the sign above the door. THE SPOILED BRAT. Yep, she was at the right place. Yep, she was meeting her sister at a gay bar. She didn't mind, but she did wish Jill had warned her. Amy had been hoping to get laid, but as she was the heterosexual of the two sisters, her prospects were diminishing rapidly.

Oh, well, she thought, it was Jill's party. Her younger sister had just graduated from UCSF and had scheduled a week of festivities before she went to Europe for the summer. *Lucky bitch,* Amy thought, laughing to herself. Jill was on a plane to London tomorrow. Amy was on a plane too, but back to L.A. for work.

Just then Jill walked up and gave Amy a slap on the butt. "Damn, Amy," she said. "You need some meat on your bony little ass!"

"Well, not everybody is built like a Mack truck!" Amy snapped back in mock pique. Jill actually had a great ass, round and muscular from years of competitive sports. Amy was built entirely differently, tall and slender to Jill's compact, athletic body. The sisters were nothing alike. Amy, older by six years, was blonde and willowy and often topped her male companions in height if she was wearing the fuck-me pumps. Tonight she was dressed in a cute little black dress that accentuated her long legs, and red shoes that matched her lipstick. Jill had short, curly brown hair, didn't own a single dress, and hardly wore any makeup. She was dressed in jeans and an old jersey.

"Shall we get this party started?" Jill said, as she opened the door. "I'll buy the first round!"

A wave of retro '80s music hit them as they entered the bar. It was dark inside, but Amy could see the crowded bar, a pool table and dartboard off to the left, and a small dance floor beyond that. Jill's girlfriend Laurie was already there, settled in with a group at a table in the back. Amy had already met most of them at Jill's graduation ceremony, so the introductions were quick. Jill went off to secure the promised drinks, while Amy surveyed the dance floor. All the men were coupled up with other men, and she wasn't interested in women. She sighed; it would be another lonely night in her bed.

The drinks arrived, and Jill handed her what she proclaimed was a "Dark and Stormy," a specialty of the bar: ginger beer and vodka. It was refreshing after the heat outside. She drank it down quickly, and as quickly had another pushed into her hand. She knew she should take it easy, but here, surrounded by Jill's friends, she felt safe enough. And maybe drinking would keep her from thinking about Frank.

Frank was her ex-husband. Amy couldn't help smiling ruefully as she remembered his pet name for her. He had called her his spoiled brat. How ironic that she was sitting in a bar of the same name a few months later, trying to drown her memories of him.

Spoiled brat. He said he'd give her anything, but he'd only given her what he had felt like giving, never what she wanted. And all she had wanted was his love. She didn't care about jewelry or cars or the house, just him. She had pretended not to notice the "business trips" and "work dinners," not believing Frank was actually having an affair until he'd dialed the wrong number and left her a voice message that was undeniably not meant for her. When she confronted him, he had tried to turn it all back on her, accusing her of always wanting too much from him, unlike his mistress. Suddenly she wasn't a spoiled brat any more, but a greedy little bitch. Jill had been there for Amy throughout the hasty divorce, and Amy wasn't going to let it ruin Jill's party.

Amy spent the rest of the evening laughing and chatting with Jill and her friends. They were a lively bunch, if a bit rowdy, and a good distraction. It was a good time, but the crowd was slowly thinning, and one by one Jill's friends were excusing themselves. Soon only Amy, Jill and Laurie were left. Laurie pulled Jill onto the dance floor, leaving Amy by herself.

Amy's eyes wandered over the few patrons left in the bar. A couple of women dressed in denim and leather were playing pool, and some young men in tight T-shirts were laughing at a nearby table, but it was the couple slow dancing in a corner that caught her eye. Two men, each attractive in his own way: a tall blond with close-cropped hair and a smaller, wiry brunet with a neatly trimmed goatee. They were both dressed in casual business attire, like they had come straight from work. They would slow dance for a bit, then stop to kiss, hands wandering over each other. How she wished she had somebody to dance with too.

She couldn't stop watching the romantic couple. It was obvious they weren't strangers in the way they touched and the way they leaned close to talk and laugh. The blond slipped his arm around the shorter man's waist with an easy intimacy. She realized she was staring when the blond glanced up at her. She hastily looked away, blushing. She hadn't meant to be rude! She looked up just as the blond was making his way over to her table, his dance partner in tow.

"Hey there, gorgeous, would you like to dance?" Blondie asked.

"I thought you were with *him*," Amy replied, confused.

"He is," interjected the brunet playfully, "but maybe *you* could be with *us*!"

"I'm Matt," continued the blond, "and this is Andrew. We thought you looked lonely. Come dance with us!" He extended his hand, and Amy couldn't resist the twinkle in his blue eyes.

"I'm Amy," she said with a laugh. "Let's dance!"

Matt and Andrew led her out onto the dance floor. A fast song was on, and they danced in a loose circle. Amy loved to dance, and these guys were great partners. The song ended, and a slow song began. Amy was about to return to the table, but Andrew caught her hand. "I thought you were going to dance with us?" he asked, gently pulling her to him. Soon they were all slow dancing together, wrapped in a loose embrace. It seemed only natural when Andrew leaned forward to kiss her softly on the lips, but when Matt moved in to kiss her next, alarms went off in her head, and she stepped back from them.

"Wait a minute, boys," Amy said with an awkward laugh, "what the hell is going on here?"

"Don't worry," said Matt, "we don't bite. Much. But we both think you're hot, and we thought you might want some… companionship."

"I'm not sure I know what you mean," Amy stammered.

"Matt and I are going home to *fuck*," Andrew said, giggling. "We want you to come play with us!"

Amy was stunned, not so much at the proposition, but at her body's reaction to it. She couldn't deny that she was attracted to both of them, and that watching them make out had been turning her on. But seriously, she couldn't go to bed with not just one, but *two* men she had just met! Could she?

She looked around frantically for Jill, found her at the bar and silently begged for help. Jill read her panic and sauntered over. "Hey Matt, Andy, I see you've met Amy. My *sister* Amy." Jill's expression was friendly, but there was a subtle warning in her voice.

"Hey, no offense," Andrew said, lifting his hands. "But your sister is hot! We just thought she might be interested in a little fun, is all. You know we're cool."

Jill looked up at Amy. "He's right," she said. "They may be horrible sluts," she added with a laugh, "but they're good guys. If you want to go with them, I won't stop you. In fact, maybe they're just what you need!"

Amy looked at Matt and Andrew and felt a tingling between her legs as the blood rushed to her pussy. Well, she *had* been hoping to get laid tonight...

Matt went to call a taxi, and Jill left with Laurie. Amy turned to Andrew. "Do you two do this often?" she asked. "I mean, pick up women together."

"Not often," he replied, "but...well, we both noticed you, and we both wanted to fuck you. No offense, but we don't usually agree on women, so...no, we don't do this often."

"You should feel privileged," he added with a wink.

They made out in the back of the cab, Amy sitting in the middle, turning to kiss first one and then the other. *What the hell am I doing?* she thought in a panic. The thought was quickly drowned by Andrew's tongue invading her mouth as Matt slid his hand up her thigh and started massaging her crotch through her panty hose. She moaned as Andrew's fingers began squeezing her breasts, and then she was kissing Matt again.

Somehow they ended up in the two men's apartment, but Amy had no idea how they got there. She didn't think the three of them had stopped kissing for a moment. The groping and fondling had made her frantic with need, and once inside, she immediately started unbuttoning Matt's shirt. "Slow down," he whispered, "we have all night."

Matt and Andrew removed her clothes slowly, kissing and nibbling each part of her body. She whimpered when they removed her bra, freeing her aching nipples. Andrew immediately bent to suck on them, teeth gently tugging at first one, then the other. "Beautiful," he breathed. "You have beautiful tits!" Amy knew that her breasts were relatively small, but the way he was worshipping them made her feel like a goddess. A girl could get used to that!

Amy sat on the couch and watched, mesmerized, as the two men undressed, their cocks already stiffening with passion. Andrew's cock was surprisingly thick and meaty, while Matt's was slightly longer but didn't have quite the girth of Andrew's. Both were beautiful specimens, drops of precome already beading on the delicate tips. She ran her gaze over the rest of their bodies. Andrew had lighter skin, a wiry build and a tight, muscular butt. His chest was smooth, and his dark brown nipples were big and hard. Matt was a golden tan with a line of dark fur starting at his navel and pointing the way down. His strong, wide shoulders tapered to a narrow waist.

Andrew dropped to his knees to take Matt's hard member into his mouth with the practiced ease of a longtime lover. Amy was a little surprised he didn't gag. Matt's hands gripped the sides of Andrew's head, holding it still while he thrust into Andrew's waiting mouth. Amy spread her legs and started stroking her pussy as she watched. Matt glanced over and gave a strangled groan when he saw her playing with herself; she thought he was going to come right then, but he slowed to a stop.

Andrew looked at Amy with a grin. "Your turn," he said. At first Amy thought he meant it was her turn to go down on Matt, and she was more than eager to taste him, but Andrew pushed her back on the couch and knelt between her legs. His tongue pushed into her waiting pussy. "Mmm…you're so wet," he said, before diving back in. Amy gasped as he attacked her cunt, his hot tongue plunging deep inside, his hands holding her thighs spread wide. "You taste so good," he murmured. She groaned with pleasure, eyes closing as he ate her. He slipped his fingers into her, then brought them dripping to his mouth and then to hers, smearing the juice over her lips. He kissed her, and she tasted her own tangy sweetness.

Andrew returned to eating her, concentrating on her clit now. His tongue gently circled her swollen bud as his fingers played with the petals of her lips, teasing, enticing. Amy moaned and lifted her hips, begging wordlessly for more, for something to fill the emptiness inside her cunt. He teased her with his tongue a bit longer, long slow strokes up and down her slit, before making her jump with a series of hard flicks directly on her clit. Her fingers curled in Andrew's hair, much like Matt's had. She glanced over at Matt; he was staring at them, lightly stroking his erection.

Amy beckoned to Matt and he came up beside her on the couch, offering his cock to her. She opened her mouth to take him in and almost choked as he thrust deep into her throat at the same time Andrew placed a particularly wicked flick on her clitoris. She was impressed with how easily Andrew had handled Matt's cock. She was using all of her skill to take it without gagging; Matt's deep thrusts were almost more than she could manage. Her eyes were starting to water, and she knew saliva was dripping down her chin. She was glad he didn't have Andrew's thickness, or she would never have been able to do it!

Soon Andrew was on the couch too, waving his fat cock for attention. Amy pushed Matt back and turned to suck on Andrew, her mouth stretching wide to take him. She gripped Andrew's waist to set the pace, moving up and down his cock in slow, measured strokes. He was more passive than Matt, so Amy was able to work him over, kissing from base to head and down again. She used the tip of her tongue to lick at the salty precome dripping from the end, delicately probing at the little slit, then lifted his cock to lick at his balls. He softly stroked her hair while she once again took his thickness between her lips.

Matt pulled Andrew out of Amy's mouth and the two men started rubbing their cocks, hands stroking themselves and each other. Amy let her own hands drift down, one to her breasts while the other slowly fingered her slick sex. She rubbed some of her moisture over her nipples. She couldn't believe how erotic she was finding it to watch these two men pleasuring each other right in front of her face, both of their cocks glistening with her saliva. She decided to try a doubleheader and opened her mouth as wide as she could. They got the hint and pushed their cocks into her mouth. She could barely fit the two heads in, one hand around each shaft as she worked them both. She alternated going down on first one juicy cock, then the other. She felt like a kid in a candy store.

"Aren't you jealous?" Matt asked her. "Don't you want one too? Don't you want to know what it's like?"

Amy looked up at him, puzzled, but couldn't answer with Andrew's cock in her mouth. Andrew laughed and pulled back. "What he means is, don't you wish you had a penis, too?"

It was Amy's turn to laugh. She looked down between her legs. "I don't think I'm going to magically grow one any time soon!" she giggled.

"You don't have to...come with me..." Matt pulled her off the couch and led her to the bedroom. He went to the nightstand and rummaged in the drawer. "Here it is!" he said triumphantly, presenting her with a flesh-colored dildo. "Here, this goes with it." He handed her some straps.

Amy was shocked. She'd heard of strap-ons, but had never in a million years imagined herself wearing one. Then again, she had never imagined giving head to two men at the same time. Well...she had actually fantasized about that before, but had never expected it to happen!

Andrew helped her figure out the harness, one strap going between her legs and another buckling around her waist. Amy glanced down in awe to see her very own cock springing erect from her crotch. It was a very nice cock, she thought, not ridiculously large like some dildos she had seen, but a good size with a slight curve to it and a well-defined ridge at the head. Andrew got down on his knees in front of her, looking up with a grin before going down on her. She gasped as he took her in, noting the slick shine of his saliva coating her shaft. She knew it was impossible to feel the blow job, but she could swear the sensations were traveling straight down the silicone cock to her clit. She grabbed Andrew's hair, pulling him onto her, shoving it down his throat like Matt had. He moaned and attacked her cock with vigor. She felt empowered; she'd often been aggressive in the bedroom, but nothing had prepared her for the raw sense of control she felt as she watched Andrew blow her.

Amy looked up to see Matt grabbing a condom from the bowl on the nightstand. He unrolled it onto his erect member and knelt behind Andrew, grabbing him by the hips. Andrew moaned again as Matt dribbled some lube onto his ass and then slowly inserted first one, then two fingers. "Are you ready?" Matt whispered as he withdrew his fingers and rubbed the tip of his cock against Andrew's pucker. Andrew sucked even harder on Amy's cock as he nodded his head, and she watched in amazement as Matt's long cock slowly disappeared into Andrew's ass.

Matt fucked Andrew slowly, almost gently, letting Andrew widen to accommodate him, as Amy fucked Andrew's mouth. Matt's eyes met Amy's, and he asked her if she wanted a turn. He slowly withdrew from Andrew and motioned her over. He handed her a condom and the lube.

"Holy hell," she said, "I never thought I would be putting a condom on my own cock!"

"Okay now, gently at first," Matt told her. "But once he gets used to you, you can ride him harder."

"Ride him harder?" Amy squeaked. "I've never fucked anybody before! I'm not sure I know how! And.....I don't want to hurt him..."

"It's okay," Andrew said with a grin, "I'm a big boy."

Amy looked down at Andrew's ass, then at her cock, which suddenly looked a lot bigger than it had before. "Are you sure?" she asked, but she was already putting the condom on her dick. She giggled suddenly. She actually had a dick!

Andrew only smiled in answer and waggled his butt playfully. Amy caught hold of his hips as Matt had done and moved the tip of her cock into place. She leaned into him and pushed forward slowly before nervously backing off. "It's okay," he said encouragingly. She placed the tip of her member against him once more, and this time he moved backward onto it, groaning softly. "That's it," he said, "now fuck me, bitch!"

Amy laughed and proceeded to do just that, thrusting her

hips forward until her cock was in him to the hilt. She looked up to see Matt thrusting into Andrew from the other end and had a moment of concern before she realized he had discarded his soiled condom. She felt Andrew reacting to Matt's thrusts, making the dildo grind against her clit, and she gasped and thrust forward again. She saw Andrew's head being forced forward onto Matt's cock with every thrust she made. She fucked him faster and harder, the pressure on her clit and pussy becoming more intense until she was crying out with each thrust. She didn't even notice that Matt was now leaning back on his haunches to watch, cock once more in hand, or that Andrew was crying out in time with her. She grabbed Andrew's hips and pulled him back as she simultaneously slammed her thighs forward against him, over and over, until suddenly she came, in great heaving spurts. She was not at all surprised to feel her own hot jizz dripping down the inside of her thighs.

"Are you okay?" she asked shakily as she removed her cock from Andrew's ass. "Did I hurt you?"

"I'm fine," Andrew replied, just as shakily. "Damn girl, I think you're a natural!"

Amy would have blushed, but just then she felt Matt behind her, his hand on her shoulder bending her forward. "We take turns," he said. "But lady's choice, ass or cunt?"

"Pussy," she managed to gasp as Matt removed the harness fastened around her waist. Suddenly Matt was plunging into her sopping and still quivering sex. It was Andrew's turn in front, and she latched onto him with her lips, the force of Matt's fucking driving her down onto Andrew's cock. She had always wanted to be taken from both ends like this, like she and Matt had taken Andrew.

Matt reached around to finger her sensitive clit, and her second orgasm came quickly, almost a continuation of her first.

But Matt didn't stop, mercilessly rubbing her swollen bud as he continued to fuck her, setting her nerves on fire as her entire body shuddered. Her orgasm reached almost painful heights as she fought not to bite down on Andrew's cock filling her mouth. She could hear herself whimpering frantically as her thighs involuntarily tried to squeeze shut, but just as she thought she couldn't take any more, Matt started taking her back down again, slowing to a gentle stop.

Amy disengaged from both men and rolled over onto her side. "Oh, my god," she moaned. "What the fuck did you do to me? I've never come that hard in my life!"

Matt and Andrew looked at each other silently, and then Andrew spoke up. "We're not done with you yet," he said softly, "if you think you can handle some more..."

Amy looked up at them, amazed at their energy. "Some more what?" she said. "After the orgasm you guys just gave me, I'll do anything you ask me to."

"Well," Andrew said slowly, almost hesitantly. "We want to fuck you together, one from the front, and one from the back..."

"Didn't you just do that?" she asked.

"Not like that...I would be on the bottom, and you would be on top of me...and Matt would be behind you..."

"Just show me," Amy said. "That would probably be easier!"

Andrew smiled and lay on the bed on his back. "Come here, Amy," he said, and she climbed up beside him. His cock was only semihard now; after all, they had been fucking for quite a while. She decided to remedy that by going down on him for a bit, enjoying the feel of him hardening in her mouth. When he was ready, she looked up expectantly. "Climb on top," he directed, and she obeyed, positioning herself over his cock and shuddering as she eased herself down onto him. Her entire pussy was swollen and raw and dripping wet.

Matt climbed up on the bed beside Amy, and she was once again presented with his cock. This time she could taste her own cream on it. She slowly ground down on Andrew while sucking and licking her white come off of Matt's quivering member. "Kiss me," Andrew whispered, and she leaned down, the scent of her sex on both their faces. She felt Matt move behind her and heard the familiar rustling of a condom wrapper. "What..." she stammered, but Andrew pulled her back into another kiss.

"Don't worry," Matt said gently. "Relax...just relax, I won't hurt you, I promise."

Amy tried to relax. She wasn't usually too keen on anal sex, but after all the fucking they had done, she felt loose and open. She wondered vaguely if they had made her come so hard on purpose, to soften her up. She gasped as she felt Matt's lubed finger enter her hole, slowly moving in and out, then she groaned as he pushed another finger in. Below her, Andrew jerked as he felt Matt's fingers too.

"I'm ready," she whispered, trying not to tense her muscles in anticipation.

She felt the head of Matt's erection against her ass now, pushing gently, and she could feel Andrew throb inside her as Matt's cock slowly stretched her and entered her. All three of them groaned loudly as Matt slid home. He paused, letting her body adjust to him, and she was again glad he wasn't as wide as Andrew. Matt began to move in and out of her, causing both her and Andrew to moan and squirm. She couldn't believe she actually had both of those beautiful cocks in her at once. She felt stretched wider than she had ever been. Slowly their bodies ground together, the cocks filling her until Amy thought she couldn't contain it all. She started to panic for a moment, but

Andrew stroked her face. "It's okay," he said, "It gets easier." And he was right. The more she relaxed, the more she was enjoying this, the two cocks putting pressure on her G-spot from opposite directions. She felt Matt's body over her, his arms on either side of her shoulders supporting his weight. He's making love to Andrew, she thought, through me....

She could feel an orgasm growing inside her for the third time that night. She thought about the cocks inside her, how Matt and Andrew must be feeling their cocks rubbing against each other, how they both must feel every twitch of her pussy, even as she felt their every movement.

Andrew gripped Amy's hips and started thrusting up into her, and Matt's groan was her only warning before he started pounding fiercely down into her. She came like that, screaming, two cocks almost violently claiming her, claiming each other, and she realized that they were coming too, all three at once, in a frantic, urgent crescendo. Their orgasm seemed to last forever, until they collapsed into a shuddering, wet heap.

Amy woke several hours later, Matt and Andrew sprawled on the bed beside her. Matt was snoring softly. She quietly got dressed and, finding the address on a piece of mail on the kitchen counter, called a cab. She let herself out of the apartment and smiled to herself, remembering how she had fucked them; how she had taken Andrew and taken Matt; greedy lover that she was, she had taken it all. Spoiled brat, indeed.

AN AUDIENCE
OF ONE

N. T. Morley

Haley Bennett parked in a metered spot, but it was well after metering hours. She got out of her Subaru with her heart pounding, her legs feeling very weak and shaky. It wasn't just the six-inch heels she wore; she was scared. What woman wouldn't be, walking alone in a very bad neighborhood after midnight? Especially a woman in Haley's circumstances.

She was twenty-eight—a tall, pale woman with wheat-blonde hair. She had a pretty face but nothing special by Hollywood standards, which was why in twelve of her two-dozen second-rate films she'd been the best friend who made snarky comments in Act I, and in Act II was the emotional sounding board for the better-looking heroine, giving her a stern talking-to by delivering homespun wisdom the audience already knew. The closing moments always saw her looking pleased with herself at the wedding, or announcing her own engagement to the hero's geeky friend. The rest of the time, she modeled clothes in local catalogs, being flown to places like Kansas City where VIPs got

Pabst and Doritos instead of champagne and caviar. Which was more her taste, anyway.

But this time it was Haley Bennett's own movie, and she was the star. She was a hell of an actress, but there wouldn't be much acting for her to do this time—she was self-directing and all she knew to do was *Scared. Act very scared.* You might call it "method."

She looked around her, making sure there was no one within line-of-sight. A few scattered lumps in the corners represented men beneath filthy blankets, taking far less interest in Haley than their dreams. Of waking people, the street was deserted.

This neighborhood had been a densely populated urban slum, the worst in the city, until redevelopment brought cops and men with clipboards to kick out the residents packing the decaying cinder-block buildings. Temporary fences cropped up everywhere, and bulldozers came in. Many of them were still there, parked haphazardly in the open expanses of rubble that had once been homes. The dozers had been left there when the funding dried up months ago—*many* months ago, in some cases. They could have been moved back to the yard, but why bother? There was nowhere to go. Nothing new was being built, so nothing old was being demolished. Even carting away the debris was out of the question for outfits gone bankrupt. What that left was a mostly empty stretch of urban blight where looming buildings alternated with empty lots of rubble.

The alley Haley had selected, which her Subaru was now parked almost exactly one block from, was between two of those existing buildings. They had been emptied of residents, padlocked and cyclone-fenced, then left. The long, dark alley stretched down between two of those buildings, its front region lit by the street's hissing yellow sodium lamps in slanted rays that illuminated puddles of stagnant water and a strewn array of garbage. The alley dead-ended somewhere well past the point where darkness claimed it. Whether there was a vast cinder-block wall there with gang-tag graffiti, like there was at the end of most of these alleys, Haley didn't know. That part was Kend-rick's problem. All Haley knew was she was going down there.

She wore a camel-colored trench coat. The mercury was edging toward a hundred, but the surface of the coat was chilly. It was too hot to drive with a coat on.

She took a deep breath and slipped her trench coat off.

Underneath, she wore not much at all. Oh, to be sure, she would have been decent at a society function, as the trophy wife with tits and ass hanging everywhere, brassy and shameless, slutty makeup a sign of her rich husband's status and her own infinitesimal IQ, whether tactfully faked like her blonde hair or all natural like her tits. She would have been decent at a porn-star tradeshow, packed into a dress that showed her thighs, her garters, the tops of her red stockings with their cute red bows affixed to the lace tops in back, up close to the place where the hem of the dress almost—almost—showed the swelling curve where her cheeks met her thighs. She would have been decent on a strip-club stage, with ample D-cups spilling out, shoved up in a dangerous perch where the dress plunged low. She would have been decent sprawled across the bed of a pay-by-the-minute hotel room or in the bedroom of a man who had paid for her, or on a street where she intended to find one.

As Haley folded her coat and tried to put it down in the driver's seat, she panicked and looked around again. She saw two dark lurking forms in the shadows at the far end of the empty buildings on either side of her. She saw another in an alley directly across from her. Two more dark forms could be seen distantly on the outskirts of a construction site, catty-corner to her. How many? Ten? She didn't know. She *wouldn't* know, until it started. Maybe not even then. Maybe never.

She felt her heart pounding and very much wanted to run. She could have gotten in the car and fled for home, or simply looked and motioned them over and asked for a hug. But Haley had come this far, and she did not intend to chicken out now. If nothing else, doing so would mean she'd have to do it all again some other time, or spend the rest of her life wishing she had. Which is not to say if it didn't happen, she wouldn't be incredibly relieved. Having to abandon the plan because some cop car drove by would feel like a reprieve. Having to abandon it because she chickened out would feel, on the contrary, like an execution. She'd have to put all this effort in all over again from scratch, or beg and plead for everyone involved this time to forgive her and trust that she wouldn't chicken out again. And Kendrick, she knew, would never forgive her. He'd *say* he would, but he'd never take her assurances seriously after this.

She heard her own stupid voice in her head—echoes of the many conversations, her many begging, pleading entreaties. *Really*, she'd told him. *I really want to do this. I promise, it's not just a lark. And yes, I'm serious about the number. I don't just want three or four. I want ten...or twenty. As many as you can get. As long as you trust that they're reliable, and you check that their tests are real...then I'll trust you. No. I'm not going to blame you. I'm not. I know it's risky. But I want it. I have to have it. Please, baby? Please? I'll do anything for you if you make this happen. Please?*

That meant this was the very last moment she could cut and run, and it would all be over. There was no cop car to rescue her; there were no homeless people immediately in evidence to mean the site wasn't safe. The lurking forms were ready—hard already, maybe. They were standing in the shadows waiting for Haley Bennett to do as she'd been told—as she had *asked* to be told. If she did not, then it was all off.

She felt dizzy. She actually went to get back in the car, and then came to her senses. She threw down the coat and threw down her keys atop it. They landed with a clang. She slammed the door but left the car unlocked.

She started walking.

Haley moved quickly, mincing in tiny steps, feeling tottery on her high heels. She glanced around and saw dark figures following—everywhere. Places they couldn't have been. Looking at her from windows. Hovering above the street. Perched on power poles. Her heels clicked faster and faster, echoing through the canyons of the city. Panicking, she tried not to run. Her heart pounded. She felt warmth hit her skin. She felt something hot inside her. She felt the fear push her emotions into overdrive.

She reached the alley and ducked down it, into the dark as if seeking refuge from the shadows. She mini-stepped, her heels clicking louder than ever in the narrow space, as she ran toward the big black at the end of the alley, imagining for an instant that she'd gotten the wrong alley, this one wasn't a dead end, and she could slip out undetected and race back to her car. It wasn't a done deal yet; even with a safeword, she could still outsmart the shadows.

The buildings were tall and the light was distant and she was in the dark before she knew it. It's not like she wasn't expecting it, but when the huge dark form leapt at her from the blackness, she screamed.

One big hand clamped across her face as the other seized her long, blonde hair. Haley struggled and screamed again, a muffled sound behind the tightly clamped hand. Still holding her hair, the big man spun her around and grabbed her wrist; he shoved her up against a smooth concrete wall and pulled her wrist up so hard Haley yelped again, louder than ever this time.

Freed from the hand across her face, she tried to scream again—but this time the sound became a strangled groan as the hand pulled her wrist up into the small of her back and higher in a pain-compliance hold. She flailed with her other hand, weakly—but she couldn't get purchase. Haley was tall-ish—six-foot-two in these six-inch heels. The man with her wrist and her hair in his hands still sported two inches on her—in fact, she knew he was six-four exactly. She knew because she bragged about his height and his shape—like a *building*—to any girlfriend who could listen, and any asshole casting director who made off-color comments. *Oh, thank you so much for the compliment,* went her go-to brush-off. *No, I'm not offended at all. I mean, I think everyone likes to get compliments, especially when it's totally innocent. My boyfriend Kendrick—you'd really like him—he's always getting compliments. He's six-four and black, you see, and he works out five or six times a week at this gym in West Hollywood—you know the Power Punch Boxing gym? Anyway, he's always getting compliments from gay men at the gym, and he never takes offense—he really loves it. For him, he just sees it as motivation to work on his power lifting! He even has groupies! Of course, he's broken the gym's power lifting limit six times, so—hey, maybe you and he could work out together! He's in the industry, he's a stuntman and a martial arts instructor. He'll be picking me up later—I can introduce you!* Wandering hands never became a problem.

The man behind her pinned her against the wall and leaned down to press his mouth to her ear. He wore a spandex hood with eyeholes and a mouth-hole.

"You make a sound and I'll hurt you," he said. "Just be a good girl and you'll walk away. You'll be walking funny, but you'll walk away. Act up and you won't. Do you understand?"

Haley *did* understand—she'd all but *written* the script. But whether it was method acting that made terror paralyze her vocal cords—or she was just so fucking turned on she couldn't think or speak or comprehend—she didn't know. All she knew was that a hot, painful sob came bursting out of her lungs as she started to hyperventilate.

"Breathe slow and easy, slut. You've got a long night coming. Breathe slow and easy and do as you're told. You know you want this. We know you want this. You're gonna get everything you ever dreamed of, and then some. Make it nice and easy for us and we'll make sure you enjoy it. Give us any shit? We'll make sure you don't. Am I understood?"

She'd expected Kendrick's voice to calm her—but it didn't. Hearing him now, with the cold growl of pure and awful evil rumbling under him, she was left writhing in terror under his grasp: Had she miscalculated? Was her gorgeous, brilliant, sexy boyfriend of four years really a psychopath?

He sure as hell seemed like it. When she just whimpered in response, he shoved her hard against the concrete wall. She flattened her palm against the warm concrete and let out a sob.

He leaned up hard against her.

She felt his cock, hard as iron, pressing against the barely covered curve of her ass.

Deep in the alley, choked by shadows, Kendrick shoved her forward. It was so dark she couldn't even see what was in front of her, so she uttered a strangled yelp of terror as she pitched forward. She was caught not by Kendrick's hands on her wrist and in her hair, but by the hard, cold, smooth surface of an aluminum garbage can. It was exactly the right height to shove her ass up high as he forcibly bent her over. He kicked her feet apart; she yelped again as she felt herself suspended in space. Shadows flooded all around her—six, ten, a dozen, more. Men—heavy boot-steps. Ski masks. One with a camera, expensive, professional, probably "borrowed" from some locker at a documentary studio. The cameraman—a professional—pointed the lens at her ass, but never at her face. She heard the soft whir of digital video, saw the infrared blink and a green light illuminating black, blank, evil faces.

Her dress rode up above her asscheeks. Kendrick's hand slid up between her legs and he growled in vicious pleasure.

"Nothing underneath. What kind of a slut walks around in this neighborhood, dressed like this with no panties?"

He shoved two fingers inside her.

"And she's wet. Let's give her what she wants!"

There were murmurs around her as the men crowded in. One grabbed her hair out of Kendrick's hand and tipped her head back. Someone else grabbed her jawline and squeezed; when she tried to clamp her lips shut, he squeezed harder.

Someone, a stranger, unzipped his pants in front of her, just inches from her face. He pulled out his cock—enormous, dark, uncut. He pulled back his foreskin and showed her his dick—and then Haley saw nothing more, as a spandex mask was shoved over her head. It was shaped like a hood, but open at the top and the mouth to leave her cascade of pretty blonde hair available as a handhold—to facilitate the use of her mouth, which was now open and receptive.

The man who'd showed her his dick grabbed her hair and slid his huge cock into her mouth. He wasn't as rough as he could have been—Haley half wished he would fuck her so hard she would choke. But he gave her just long enough to get used to it, to straighten her throat and open wide for the dick about to ravish her face.

Then he shoved his dick down her throat, and Haley swallowed it easily, feeling a hot rush as she was "forced" to take cock down her throat.

Behind her, Kendrick had his hands deep in her. Or could it have been someone else? There were so many men all around her—a dozen, two dozen, three, four, five; it could have been a hundred. How many men had Kendrick recruited? She would never know, not even when she saw the video later. She would just know that she had been taken by many, and it was safe. Whether it was Kendrick who first took her wasn't the point. The point was that *all* of them took her—bent over a garbage can in a dark alley.

Her dress was pulled up hard, above her waist. The garbage can shuddered. She could feel it was filled with sand—her idea, stuntman tested!—and had had all the sharp edges filed off or taped over.

She heard the camera whining slightly as the cameraman came in close and got a nice shot of her ass and her pussy; her cheeks were held open for the camera. She felt the stranger's cock going rhythmically down her throat and felt her pussy lips being parted.

Naked, hard dick eased up and down her slit, teasing her open—then it came. The first thrust. A hard *shove*. So hard it would have hurt, if she hadn't been ready for it and hungry for it and pouring like a gusher. She tried to raise her ass to meet it and felt a hot wave of fear as hands and dicks and body weight held her down and cocks plunged rhythmically down her throat and into her cunt.

She felt her orgasm building.

That was, of course, not at all possible. No way could she be ready to come so fast. She'd been in a state of arousal for *weeks* as Kendrick planned this thing with her feedback; she hadn't been masturbating because she was too afraid to accept that it would really happen—but too obsessed to slip into an alternate fantasy. When she and Kendrick made love he tried to talk to her about it, and she shushed him and said let's talk about something else.

Her pent-up energy was uncontrollable; the hard dick sliding bareback into her cunt was more than enough to bring her off after two minutes, three at the most. Her violent struggles made the man in her mouth slide his dick out and slap her face with it; that meant her mouth was free and her throat open as she howled in what only a fool could fail to see was an explosive, soul-searing orgasm.

She let out a sob of pleasure, her body subsumed by the waves of satisfaction rolling through her. A ripple of laughs and cheers went through the crowd, and she heard Kendrick's voice among others saying, "Slut," "Whore," "Wanted it," "Give her what she wants." His voice was distant; it was a stranger using her now. A stranger's cock had just made her come. Dizzy with that knowledge, Haley felt her face go red and hot with shame and arousal. The men crowded in with new gusto. Her dress, already soaked through with sweat, was pulled up higher and ripped open in front so new men could feel her tits, pinch her nipples. The man in front of her slid his cock back down her throat, and Haley opened wide.

Was it two hours later? Three? Four? Five? The sun was not up, so it could not have been six, but it felt like it—her gang bang a lost, swirling mass of smells and tastes and cocks and hands and big heavy bodies pinning her down. A whirl of orgasms, too many to count. She didn't know how long it had been as they hauled her off the garbage can, her dress ruined, her legs and masked face streaming come, spit, sweat and her own juices.

But even a girl who wants it can only take so much.

Someone had retrieved her trench coat. They propped her up and slid it onto her, moving her arms for her because she was well beyond it. Kendrick left her hood on as he carried her to the car. He put her in the passenger's seat and gave her a towel, but she was far too tired and horny even to wipe herself. They'd take care of that once he got her home.

She heard faint voices outside—Kendrick uttering thanks, and slapping men on their backs for fucking his girlfriend. She felt her pussy trembling, twitching; how many times had she come? Too many. Too many to take. No sex would ever compare; she was sure of it. Except maybe the thank-you sex she'd have with Kendrick—that she intended to have with Kendrick, however he wanted and whatever he wanted, whenever, always, forever. He was golden to her in that moment: the man who had given her what she wanted. Finally.

There was plenty of night left. She'd later see *01:16:06* on the closing seconds of the raw videotape, as she was carried to the car soaked with come. She'd watch it over and over again, orgasming, buzzing herself with a vibrator or just rubbing fast with her hand. For a year, she'd watch her ravishment daily— with Kendrick and by herself. For a year after that, she'd watch it weekly. Then it would always be there, to remind her how much Kendrick loved her. Eventually it would be kept in a fire-proof safe, to keep it away from their kids.

Would this get out some day and ruin her career?

She didn't really care. Scandal in Hollywood is cheap, and she was far too obscure to rate more than a line in a scandal sheet. One of the men would have to have recognized her before the hood went on, or put the pieces together afterward. And even if it ever did get out, she felt strongly that it would be worth it.

Haley Bennett had gotten what she wanted—a chance to give the performance of a lifetime.

And didn't all actors, ultimately, perform for an audience of one?

CHOCOLATE CAKE

I. G. Frederick

Louise sat down on the worn sofa next to Maria and crossed one leg over the other. She set her mocha grande on the small rickety table at her elbow.

Freedom of Espresso didn't have the most comfortable furnishings, but they made the best mochas in Renton. Louise always tried to indulge at least once on those rare occasions that she ventured back to the Seattle area.

"So, what have you been up to since I've seen you. Gracious, it's been years. Are you dating anyone?"

"Not exactly."

At that moment, Louise noticed a tall, dark-haired man wearing an emerald-green linen shirt that emphasized a muscular chest and powerful arms. He stood near the end of the coffee bar a few feet away. His eyes ran the length of Louise's legs from the strappy sandals up her firm calves to where her tanned thighs disappeared under her shorts. His gaze continued upward taking in her narrow waist and the cleavage displayed by her half-buttoned silk shirt.

She reached over with her left hand for her coffee cup. The man's eyes followed her movement and a smile played across his lips. He stepped to the side of the sofa, crouched down, and said in a soft voice impossible for anyone else to overhear among the coffee shop chatter: "I couldn't help noticing the ring you wear." He looked at the gold triskelion on the middle finger of Louise's left hand and then up into her eyes. She found herself staring into the greenest pair she had ever seen. "May I assume you know the meaning of the emblem?"

Despite his quiet tone, his deep voice resonated through Louise. She nodded.

He reached out and traced the borders of the three inter-locking patterns on the ring's face with one finger. "And that you wear it on your left hand deliberately?"

She nodded.

"Do you ever get involved with dominant males?"

Louise raised one eyebrow above the other.

He leaned closer and brought his lips near enough to her ear that she could feel his breath hot on her skin. "I am not submis-sive in any way, however I find strong, powerful women can be a real turn-on for certain"—he cleared his throat—"games. And I think you're very, very attractive." He let his gaze linger on her breasts and the two tiny keys that hung between them on the gold chain around her neck.

Louise turned her head so she could whisper in his ear. She inhaled the scent of male musk unembellished with any artifi-cial odors. "I find strong, powerful men can be a real turn-on for certain games and you're very attractive, as well. But, unfor-tunately I don't live here anymore, and I catch a flight early tomorrow morning for home."

The man smiled, revealing an even row of white teeth. "I

don't want to interrupt your conversation any longer and I need to get back to the office for a quick meeting. But I would love to buy you a farewell dinner this evening. If I give you my phone number, would you call me when you're done here? I work around the corner and could return within a few minutes."

Louise had planned to spend her final evening in town with her parents. She narrowed her almost black eyes a little. "If you give me your phone number, I'll call it later this evening. But I'm afraid I won't have time for dinner. A drink after, perhaps."

He stood up, went to the counter, grabbed a napkin, scribbled on it, stepped back to the sofa and handed it to Louise. "This is my cell. I'd love to hear from you anytime before you leave town."

Louise looked at the phone number, folded the napkin and tucked it into the breast pocket of her shirt.

"May I ask who will be calling me?"

"Lady Louise."

He reached down, took her hand in his, brought it to his face and touched his lips to her ring. "Sir Peter so looks forward to hearing from Lady Louise."

He rose and grabbed a paper cup from the end of the coffee bar. The bells above the door tinkled as he left.

Maria stared at Louise. "Whatever were you two whispering about? Was that someone from your sordid past?"

Louise shook her head. "No, just wishful thinking on my part." She savored the complex chocolate and coffee mixture and wondered how Peter had picked up on her inconsistencies.

"So, I suppose there's no possibility of you hooking up with that guy later, falling in love and moving back up here?" Maria sipped from her clear plastic cup filled with ice and creamy Italian soda. "I've missed you."

Louise laughed. "He's hardly my type."

"Since when is gorgeous hunk of manhood not your type?" Maria tilted her head to one side. "And what did you mean when you said you were 'not exactly' seeing anyone?"

Lowering her eyes to her cup to avoid Maria's gaze, Louise inhaled the fragrant steam. She and Maria had been best friends since high school. But she couldn't envision ever confiding that the preferred term for her current relationships was "in service" rather than "dating."

"Let's just say that I'm not looking for anyone at the moment." Even that wasn't completely truthful. Although two men competed daily with each other for the honor of fulfilling her every whim, the keys she wore were to the padlocks that kept their cocks encased in plastic. And sometimes she wanted more than a male who would lick her for hours on end or take her strap-on in his ass.

Louise knew it wouldn't be hard to sidetrack Maria if she encouraged her to talk about her own relationship. "Tell me about Jonathan." By the time Maria had shared every detail of her life with her new beau, their allotted two hours had slipped away.

Louise negotiated her rental car back toward Bellevue. While waiting in traffic, she kept thinking about how strong Peter looked. During dinner, she managed to forget about him long enough to hold up her end of the conversation with her parents and brother. But as soon as the meal ended, she excused herself. "My flight leaves early, I need to pack and get some sleep. I'll probably be gone before any of you get up in the morning, so I'll say good-bye now."

Once in her room, Louise pulled out the napkin and her cell phone. She dialed *67 before the number Peter had given her to mask her own.

"Good evening, this is Peter." His deep voice resonated

through her and she imagined his hot breath caressing her neck.

"Hi. It's Louise."

"My dear Lady, I'm so very glad to hear from you. I hope you can spare some time for me before you depart for destination unknown."

Louise looked at her watch. "My flight leaves Sea-Tac in twelve hours. I need about half an hour to pack and another half an hour or so to drive to somewhere near there."

Peter chuckled. "You do me great honor, dear Lady. May I be so bold as to book a room at the Hilton?"

"I'll meet you in the restaurant there in an hour." Louise ended the call. Most of her things were already in her suitcase—the drawers in her parents' guest bedroom were full of their off-season clothing. She changed into her travel outfit: closed sturdy shoes, jeans instead of shorts, and a denim jacket over the silk shirt. Not exactly sexy, but practical. Retrieving her toiletries from the bathroom, she stuffed them into her oversized purse.

Her brother had already left for his home in Everett, and she could hear her parents settling in for the night. Louise unmade the bed so it would look slept in and snuck out the back door with her luggage. At the bottom of the hill, she hesitated. What was she thinking, sneaking out of her parents' house to drive to a hotel and meet a man with whom she had exchanged a couple of hundred words in a coffee shop? Yet she headed toward the freeway entrance rather than return to the house. She pulled into the hotel parking lot with just enough time to make a pit stop before sashaying into Spencer's.

The moment she entered, Peter jumped up from where he lounged in one of the overstuffed armchairs across from the host stand. He kissed her hand and the touch of his lips on her fingers sent a charge of electricity racing through her, leaving every nerve tingling. Why had she decided to meet him in the restaurant rather than just go to a room? Oh, yes, negotiations. When he released her hand, she stuck both in her jacket pockets and stiffened her spine. They followed a waiter to a corner booth at the back of the dimly lit restaurant.

"Since you've already eaten dinner, how about dessert? They have a marvelous chocolate and fudge cake, perhaps with a glass of port?"

Louise smiled. "Chocolate cake yes, port no." She slid into the booth, deliberately staying near the edge, forcing Peter to sit opposite her, a large round candle flickering in between them.

When the waiter returned, he set a large piece of chocolate cake centered in a pool of hot fudge with a scoop of vanilla ice cream on one side and whipped cream on the other, in front of Louise. Peter slid around the table to sit next to her and picked up one of the two spoons from the plate. "I was hoping you'd share."

She nodded and dipped her own spoon into the cake, scooping it up with some of the fudge, ignoring the sweet white accompaniments.

"Besides," he said, as he dug into the ice cream, "I don't think you want our discussion shared with the waitstaff." He winked.

Louise let the velvety chocolate melt on her tongue and savored its richness.

"Perhaps you'd like to specify exactly what types of games you enjoy playing with dominant males?" His hot breath against her skin sent waves of desire through her.

Louise grounded herself with another mouthful of chocolate delectability before responding. "I don't like pain. Bondage is okay, if it's not too tight. I won't accept any form of humilia- tion play, you can't tear my clothing, and I do not do anything submissive." She turned to stare at him while she stuck her tongue out to lick the chocolate off her spoon with the tip of her tongue in slow sensuous strokes. "But you're bigger and stronger than I am, and I couldn't stop you from fucking my brains out, even if I tried."

Peter's smile made his eyes sparkle in the candlelight. "I see. Any physical limitations or medical conditions I should be aware of?"

She shook her head.

"Anal?"

She grimaced and shook her head more vigorously.

"Oral?"

Louise sunk her teeth into another spoonful of cake. "I bite anything that goes into my mouth."

"Gags?"

She shrugged. "Ambivalent."

"Hair pulling?"

"No pain."

He reached behind her and his fingers caressed the back of her neck. Then he bent them into her hair, and pulled her head back onto his shoulder. "This okay?"

Louise felt herself getting wet. She could never understand the pleasure she took in this type of sex. She controlled every facet of her world, including the lives of the two men in her service. But sometimes, when the right man made himself available, she just liked to let go and let him take over. She smiled.

Peter leaned over and captured her lips with his own. His tongue took possession of her mouth and she pushed closer. He pulled away, frowning. "I thought you would fight me off."

She opened her eyes wider. "Not here."

"Safeword?"

She couldn't think of anything and wondered if she would

be able to use one when he had already gotten her so aroused. "Chocolate cake."

Hot breath on her ear made it difficult to parse his next words. "Then let's go upstairs."

She nodded. Peter pushed her out of the booth, his hand still caught in her hair. He tossed a folded-up bill on the table, grabbed her purse and guided her through the nearly empty restaurant toward the elevators. When the doors slid shut, he pressed her against the wall with his body and kissed her again, hard. His hand slid inside the waistband of her jeans and his fingers found their way between her legs. He chuckled deep in his throat when he discovered how wet she'd become, his laughter rumbling in his chest.

He strode down the hallway of the fifth floor pushing Louise in front of him. She struggled to keep pace, worried someone might misinterpret their body language. Before she could even see the room number, he had a door open and was thrusting her inside. He paused long enough to turn the safety latch and toss her purse onto the desk chair. Then, he threw her onto the softness of the bed. She tried to get up, but he flipped her over on her stomach and used his belt to bind her wrists behind her back. She twisted away, but that only made it easier for him to remove her shoes and unbutton her jeans.

"No," she shouted. "Stop."

"Hell, no." Peter's voice had deepened and sounded ominous, sending a thrill of fear down her spine. "You're mine until your flight leaves, assuming I'm done with you by then." He pulled her jeans and panties off together.

She tried to crab walk away from him, but he grabbed her ankles and yanked her legs apart. Using his pelvis to hold her in place, he unbuttoned her shirt and undid the front hook on her bra. Still clothed, he used his weight to keep her from escaping while he sucked on one nipple and forced his hand in between her legs. He rubbed her slick clit with his thumb until she stiffened, close to the brink. He stopped and she screamed in frustration.

"What makes you think I have any intention of letting you enjoy this?"

She opened her mouth to answer and he stuffed her panties, fragrant with her own musk, between her teeth, cutting off her response. Before she could spit them out, he tied them in place with a bandana. Still on top of her, he grabbed both her breasts, pinching her nipples between his thumb and middle finger. She squirmed, but he stopped just before pleasure turned to pain.

Damn, he's good, she thought in a moment of lucidity. "Stop it you bastard," she mumbled around the gag, making sure she could still safeword if she needed to. She very much doubted that would be necessary.

Without getting off of her, Peter managed to remove his pants and she heard the reassuring rip of a condom package, one thing she'd forgotten to mention downstairs. He shoved himself into her so hard, her head pushed into the down pillows leaning up against the wooden headboard. Her breasts jiggled up and down with his thrusts and once again, she found herself near the edge. She attempted to disguise her approaching orgasm by trying to squirm away, but he pulled out, leaving them both panting.

"Absolutely no way." He flipped her over on her belly and piled the pillows under her stomach. "Not gonna happen."

Louise cried out, desperate for relief. Every inch of her skin burned with heat, her swollen clit ached, and her juices had soaked the bedcover and made her thighs sticky. Peter slammed into her again. She went limp, letting him fuck her, letting the tension build, she hoped, unnoticed. It took longer in this position, but his cock massaged her G-spot, pushing her toward the edge again. When he pulled out this time, she sobbed.

"You're one hot little number aren't you?" He ran his palm across her asscheeks. "Maybe I need to throw you in the shower to cool you down."

Louise knew no amount of cold water would ease the heat between her legs. She tried to rub her clit against the bed, but the pillows positioned her so she couldn't get any contact.

"No, you don't." He flipped her back over.

Pissed, she kicked at him, but he caught her leg with one hand. He produced a leather cuff with the other and buckled it on, then grabbed her other ankle. She discovered the cuffs were attached to chains. Her legs were now pointing at either corner of the bed and she had very little range of motion. Straddling her waist, his still-erect cock on her stomach, he reached behind her and removed the belt. He took off the rest of her clothing and produced two more cuffs. She tried to prevent him from capturing her wrists, twisting her upper body, pulling her arms out of his grasp twice. But her strength was no match for his, especially with her legs already bound.

He ran his hands up the length of her legs, across her hips, and up to her breasts. She squirmed. She needed to come so badly, she'd do almost anything to get relief. Except beg. He pulled his own shirt over his head without bothering to unbutton it and lay down on top of her. She pushed her hips up into him, but he kept his cock on her stomach, out of reach.

Laughing, he kissed her neck, her breasts, and nibbled on her ears. He dry-humped her belly and for a moment, she feared he would come that way. Finally, when she worried that she would pass out from frustration, he slid back into her. He rammed himself in and out of her so hard, the bed shook and the headboard banged against the wall. The tension that had been building in her clit all evening became the only thing that registered in her consciousness. The heat of his skin against hers, his heavy breathing, the pressure from his cock thrusting into her, all just pushed at that tension. She couldn't hide what was happening any more than she could shove him away and get off the bed. Her whole body stiffened, her pussy twitched and pulsed and she exploded, sobbing with relief and ecstasy. She was vaguely aware of him shuddering inside her and the pounding of his heart against her chest. When her breathing had slowed to normal, he kissed her. She didn't remember him removing the gag, but she kissed him back. She had never had such an intense orgasm in her entire life.

Somehow, the cuffs were removed and she ended up under the down comforter, snuggled in his arms with her head on his shoulder, her pussy still twitching.

"My flight..." Panic surged through her for a moment.

He stroked her hair. "Don't worry pet, I set the alarm. You can get a couple of hours' sleep."

She snuggled closer and closed her eyes.

TOURNAMENT

Abby Abbot

I do it for the money. That's what I tell people—*University isn't cheap,* I say, *a girl's gotta eat.* But what I really get off on is something else entirely.

I guess I'm rare. Whatever people say as to why they're attracted to someone—personality, intelligence, yadda, yadda, yadda—looks usually have something to do with it. But I couldn't care less. I never see my partners, and I don't want to.

Tonight I have an especially exciting partner.

All right, I'll clarify. I play chess. Competitively, online. And I'm good. I know, I know it's not cool. People say, *Why don't you go out in the evenings, Anna? You're a good looking girl, why stay inside on the Internet?* But I've got no interest in going to a bar and making small talk. What I love—lust for—is competition, pitting myself against someone else. It's a kick, trying to second-guess and outmaneuver a stranger. The money's a sideline, though I do love taking it from people.

And here's the thing: it makes me wet.

Hey JazzStar, r u ready? I type.

Hey girl. I'm always ready 2 take u.

My body temperature rises. JazzStar has never beaten me. But he's come close and we both know it. The timer blinks zero onscreen, ready to set off, and my palms are already warming. You see, it's always just possible that this time the power will tip the other way.

JazzStar moves the first pixelated pawn over the green board; the timer starts.

There's not much instant messaging banter as we play. That's not the point. I focus on planning my moves. Also on my own tension. What I know of JazzStar's game-play is that he's a fast learner, and that's nearly caught me out before. Anticipation is such a huge part of this game. It's a delicious feeling, suddenly realizing that the metaphorical rug's about to pulled out from under me and then righting myself triumphantly at the last second. Why wouldn't it?

When I take his first pawn I ease in my chair with plea-sure. Is it wrong that this arouses me too? Because my desk is up against the window I can look out into the student rooms opposite. To anyone peering in I look so conscientious, tapping away at my essays into the night. What they don't know is that beneath the desk my legs are spread wide, all the better for me to grind myself against the chair.

JazzStar takes one of my rooks. I sacrifice two pawns and am rewarded by capturing a bishop.

Gud move, JazzStar types. I revel in that, slip my hand down to my jeans. JazzStar doesn't know I do this while we play.

Three moves along my opponent unexpectedly surrounds one of my bishops, or at least I see that he will if I don't make a quick evasion. I did not see that coming; my breath catches in my throat and the flash of danger enthralls me. But I figure my way out and, pleased at my own cunning, reward myself with a quick rub of my thumb through my denim. We both promote pieces and I'm getting warmer. Christ, I hope my roommate stays out long enough for me to finish this. As JazzStar considers a retaliation I ease open the sash window and let some cool air waft over me. One of the students in the room opposite catches my eye; as I sit back down I unzip my fly and wriggle down my jeans, holding back my grin. I keep my right hand working my virtual players while my left plays with my slick cunny. JazzStar keeps slipping out of my traps tonight. Each time I'm nearly caught it heightens my arousal with this twisted power-play. Here I go, inserting ring finger, middle finger, forefinger and thumb, one at a time and back and forth and—

The doorknob screeches from behind me, and here I am so close. I'm so caught up I slam the laptop lid down, so that when my roommate enters she thinks she's caught me looking at porn. My trousers are down and I'm flushed as a summer apple. Damn.

JazzStar doesn't return for days. When he does he interrupts another game I'm playing while I'm hunched at one of the long desks in the library, keenly missing my privacy and wanking in a figurative sense only—my roommate had had keen words with me about "working" in our room again.

U withdrew, he types.

Did not! I reply, feeling a flush flood me. *Got interrupted.*

U withdrew, he repeats.

Play again? I ask. God alive, it's good he can't feel my heat through the ethernet. If we play, maybe I can hold myself till the end, then sneak into the toilets to relieve myself. I'll have to be damn quiet.

I'll let u off, if u play Thursday.

Why Thursday? I think, but type, *OK.*

Face2Face.

I draw my breath. This is breaking my rules.

Nuh-uh.

Scared?

I shift in my seat; the student sitting next to me glances up.

I always win, I type. My fingers are trembling—all right, they're shaking.

Yeah.

How should I read that? Plain acknowledgment? Or sarcasm? Is he saying the game would run differently if we met? Would it be...closer?

Not poss.

I'm passing thru.

How does he know where I am? Ah, my university email address. A giveaway.

Pub by the coach station @ 7.

And then his online status clicks to offline. I feel my heart hammering as temptation nags me. I know I'm good player. But what if JazzStar's been losing deliberately? Playing me? The possibility is so intoxicating that my legs totter as I exit the library.

I am dressed to kill because I make my own advantages. The pub is mostly locals, and I turn heads as I enter. I like that. And it's no trouble to recognize JazzStar because he's got a chess set all set up and ready. It can't be a pub set because it's complete and well cared for. I knew he was pro. Turns out JazzStar is a man after all. I slide into the seat opposite, in the eaves along-side a staircase to the upper rooms.

"This is a first," I say with a smile. Like I said, I don't care for looks, but I'll describe him. JazzStar is a man fifteen, maybe twenty years older than myself. This gives me a kick already; I know I can hold my own against players twice my age but visual proof is good. His chin is pointed like the man in the moon's, he has full lips—something my roommate once complained she finds a complete turn-off—and groomed eyebrows. He's in a suit.

"So you're a businessman, then?"

"You sound surprised."

His voice is slightly deeper than I'd imagined. We measure each other up, openly.

"I still didn't withdraw," I say.

"Huh." He leans back, grinning.

"You know, we normally play for money."

"And I thought it was for the thrill of pitting our wits."

Instinctively I cross my legs under the table—I wonder if he sees.

"That too. I just figured you'd like to know how confident I am." I flash a wad of my student loan and am pleased to see JazzStar's eyebrows rise appreciatively. "Shall we start?"

As we play a crowd gathers. The pieces gather at the sides of the board. So do the glasses—people keep buying us drinks. We keep them mostly virgin. Hell, I'm intoxicated enough. Normally, I'm meditative about my moves, taking my time to ensure I'm doing the correct thing, drawing out my pleasure. But we're beating our pieces on faster and faster, pushing our pawns up the ranks. My play increasingly takes on the feeling of wanking in front of the open curtains. I see a line of moisture form above JazzStar's full top lip, feel the crackle of escalating aggression between us. Damn, it's such good foreplay. How can anyone mistake the vibe humming over the table?

In a disastrous move I lose my queen early in the game. The crowd, the ones who know what is going on, gasp. Even JazzStar looks surprised. As I take my next move, my fingers are shaking.

But there's still that buzz telling me that the stakes are raised, I can pull this off. Between our alternating attacks a bishop disappears, two knights and several pawns. But I'm the first to get a pawn to the eighth rank on the board. JazzStar gives me a quick look. I get to promote this pawn now to another piece. Of course, there's the obvious one to choose. I choose my most powerful missing piece. That move's called queening.

And then I lose. I'm not quite sure how. Everyone seems shocked at the sudden end, the crowd, me even. The bar bell tolls for chucking-out time.

"Did you do that on purpose?" asks JazzStar.

I find I can't speak. Honestly, I don't know what I'd tell him.

"So what happens now?" asks one of the crowd.

"I don't know," I say. I feel my mouth has formed in a small smile. Then it hardens. "Rematch," I demand. But the bell tolls again. "Rematch," I repeat. And JazzStar stares hard. I don't want this to end yet.

"Everyone out," calls the barman.

"You're staying here, right?" I nod my head at the ceiling.

"Yes."

"Rematch. Upstairs."

The crowd, which has been easing away at the sound of the bell, shifts differently now. No surprise; the atmosphere above the board is almost so think you can taste it. Surely they think they see where this is going.

Who cares what they think?

JazzStar set out the board again quickly in his room. There is one chair; he takes it. The board goes on the bedside table he drags round, and I'm left to perch on the end of the bed. I doubt the connotations are being lost on either of us but even so, the game is the priority.

"You don't like losing," he comments.

"Damn straight I don't."

"But...?"

"A close fight's better," I admit after a heartbeat.

Move, move, move, move: barely studying the board, studying each other's facial expressions. Move, move, move. The room is warm and stifling. Promotion at the eighth rank. His queen captures my king.

"You're doing this on purpose," he says.

"No way."

Move, move, move. My mouth is as dry as a desert. I can't remember the last time I went this long playing without pleasuring myself too. When another piece of his reaches the eighth rank, ready for promotion, he says, incredulous, "You're going to lose again. You're doing this on purpose."

I shake my head; I can barely speak. "I just like to draw out the game. Promote your piece."

He moves to make it a queen, then stops. "No."

"No?"

"I refuse." He's breathing hard.

"Then *you* withdraw?"

"I didn't say the game's over." He stares at me. I think I'm getting the gist; my heart's in my mouth. Chess: always think ten steps ahead. Of all the permutations I can read in his eyes, and his in mine, this is surely going one way.

"Stand up," he snaps.

"What?" My authority's being challenged. Do I like this? I wonder.

"Stand up."

My legs spring up, showing themselves eager. JazzStar flicks a wild look at the tiny room, then almost pushes me to one side as he heaves against the mattress. What's he doing? Going to take me on the floor? Again, I can't decide if it's prickling excite-

ment or trepidation coursing over my skin, and the uncertainty
is electrifying. The mattress comes off, smashing a light on the
stand. Metal springs show strung between the low, dark wood
slats of the bed, like a network. JazzStar forces the mattress sideways against a wall. A thought occurs, so delicious it catches in
my throat, but then I'm distracted: the chessboard topples.

"The game!"

"Sit." And he really is breathing heavily. My legs almost give
anyway.

"You can't take your move—"

"I'm taking it now."

And it occurs: red-hot anticipation spreads over me as my legs
sink against the hardwood. It's all in keeping with the game.

Queening.

JazzStar—the man I know only through brief typed conversations, who could be anyone on earth—takes one pace forward
and rips down my skirt, panties and all. Before I can react he
dives beneath the bed in this small, rented room. When his
hands reach up through the slats a jolt like he's attached live
wires to me shakes me, because we've never touched before.
He even groans as he touches me—what a turn-on! His hands
rub against the insides of my thighs like he can't get enough,
smooth hands that reflect his desk-and-keyboard lifestyle, and
it occurs what power I have now that I'm above him. I hear him
breathe deeply in through his nose—god, I must be reeking of
desire by now. I press down against the slats and springs and his
fingers press against me as he lifts his head up and his tongue,
that tongue I've been watching ever more interestedly as this
evening's progressed, whips out against my cunny lips.

"Oh, Christ!"

It has been almost three hours of foreplay, if you don't count
the four days building up to this. JazzStar licks me again and

then starts kissing: quick, deep kisses ranging from the mouth of me up to almost where my clit is and down to the soft patch of skin in front of my anus, like he can't get enough of me. I rock forward, trying to match his rhythm but he's going too fast and desperate for me to catch him. Ahead on the carpet, his erection is standing proud through that suit of his. It must be agonizing; the idea that it might be frustrating him warms me.

"Suck me," I command, nearly growling, the way I've always wanted to command someone.

JazzStar obeys. He takes each lip gently into his mouth. I feel this oh-so-sweet tug first on one side, then the other, and he even tries to suck my clit. It turns out I'm not so good at being a remote commander because I can't help but reach my arms reach through the bed to cradle his neck—it must be aching, not that it's an entirely selfless gesture on my part. I slip my hands down his collar, needing to feel the sweat on his skin. I dig my nails in and can tell he enjoys it by the way his body arches. I repeat this and he gasps, mouth full of me. He pants warmly against those most sensitive parts. "Suck harder."

As obvious as his pleasure is, I feel I'm winning this game. Perhaps that's not so fair, as I have so much advantage. It's near torture easing myself up from his lips but I do. I catch his eye and it seems like we're so in tune mentally; he shrugs himself out from under the bed and I resume my position atop him, except now I go down to touch my lips against his cotton-clothed cock.

"Don't you fucking withdraw from this one," he gasps, grabbing air from outside the sweet prison of my crotch. "Don't you—"

He comes wonderfully, bloody fiercely, despite the fact that my lips haven't even touched any flesh of his. But his coming is enough to wipe out any holds I've been putting up against myself, and I let the waves roll in, calling out against his salt-stained trousers.

In a little while I ask, wiping a little juice from my mouth and feeling very distant, "Who won?"

"I think—it's a draw." He manages to lift his head a fraction to look at me. "Can you deal with that, competition-queen?"

I nod weakly.

It's a small university town so everyone—friends and classmates included—knew soon enough that I'd gone up to an older man's room and not come down, though most probably thought I was dull enough that it really had just been another chess match. JazzStar hasn't been on the games site since then. I think he'll come back under a different user name. So far I've not played anyone with his style but I'm still enjoying my other, lesser tournaments.

I do it for the money. Mostly.

ROCK STAR REWARDS

Rachel Kramer Bussel

Anyone who tells you that fame is the biggest perk of being a rock star is lying; sure, there's the high of being onstage, the rush of hearing your song on the radio, the fact that I never have to commute on a subway train at eight in the morning again. There's the fact that I can dye my naturally red hair an even more fiery shade of red/orange/bad-ass and get applauded, not sent to HR. There's meeting celebrities, even going to the White House once, and travel galore, and knowing that every day I get to see my art not boxed up or hanging on a wall, but alive, being hummed or sung or danced to. I love entertaining people, love being able to take my thoughts and feelings and turn them into a rock song that goes beyond words. But best of all, I love the boys who love me back.

Okay, "love" is overstating the case. I hunger for the boys who lust after me; they're men, really, but I like to call them boys, even to their faces, and they like it too. They, my groupies, are the biggest perks of the job, by far. The kind of fan a six-foot-one, Amazonian, tattooed, screaming redhead lead singer (of my band Fiery) gets aren't exactly the type who'll object to anything. I once had a boy come backstage who I told I wanted my own personal tattooer to put my name on his ass. No sooner had I said it than this sweet young thing dropped his pants! Even I don't have an on-call tattooer, and I wouldn't have gone through with it anyway; I just wanted to see what he would do.

We tour about ten months of the year; I've chosen band-mates who like the itinerant lifestyle as much as I do. Two of them, Steffy and Craig, are actually in committed relationships, while Benny is like me, the kind of guy who just goes with the flow. We're in a city one night, maybe two, and we don't form attachments, except to each other. We're not lovers, though we have been known to take a tumble on the rare night when there just aren't any groupies to our liking or we want a warm body to curl up next to far from home.

Usually, though, what happens is something like what happened tonight. Our gigs typically end around midnight, and then the real show starts. Sometimes while I'm onstage, I'll let my eyes roam over the audience and try to pick out a boy who just looks like he'd be the perfect fuck. You might think that I'm not discriminating, but that's far from true. I have stan-dards, especially because this guy's only gonna get one shot to perform. You don't want someone so insecure or uncertain that he shoots too soon or can't get it up. I want a guy who's turned on by my power, but not so turned on that he can't access his own, if fucking is on my agenda.

If I do spot a candidate, I'll have our roadie, Genius (his nickname for himself, but one that, with his voluminous store of random knowledge, we've had to concede is pretty accurate), go pull the guy aside and give him a backstage pass. Does that sound sleazy? Well, so be it. Nobody's complaining. I look for boys who I can toss around my hotel room; who I can pick up, throw across the bed, maybe take over my lap and spank. You work up a lot of adrenaline, not to mention aggression, when you're onstage, and even playing the shit out of my beloved electric guitar isn't always enough to get it all out of me. Besides, the guitar won't fuck me back. These boys will.

Sometimes I think I should've been born a guy; I'm told I talk like one, cuss like one and even fuck like one, but I don't wish I were a guy. I like being a loudmouthed, smart-ass wild girl. I like being unpredictable, and I love having a new specimen of manhood to play with every night.

There is a magic to getting to start over, to have an unfamiliar human body at your fingertips, waiting to be explored. Tonight, it was Jacob. He was twenty-five, but looked a few years younger. He had black stubble set against his pale skin, and was wearing a slightly worse for wear T-shirt of ours from five years ago, along with black jeans that had seen better days, and black and silver sneakers. I cared more about the look on his face than the look of his clothes, and what I saw when Jacob stood before me was pure adoration, like he was ready to worship me in every way. He already was, in a sense, as I flung myself all over the stage, flitting my eyes back to him on occasion. He clearly hadn't brought a girl to the show, and his eyes seemed to bore into me.

If I were looking for a soul mate, I, like other women, might have a whole checklist of things I wanted to know: job, pedigree, hobbies. But since all I wanted was some fun for the one night I was in town, a way to let off steam, to keep on seeing that worshipful face after I'd gotten off the stage, I didn't care about all that. What I cared about was how looking at Jacob made me feel: sexy, hot, invincible. During sex, I like to feel the way I do onstage, like the ruler of my own mini-universe. When

I winked at Jacob, I saw the small gesture make its way through him; he knew what it meant, he knew what I wanted. After so long in this business, I can spot my special submissives easily.

There was no band T-shirt that said, "I want to be ordered around and made to lick a powerful woman's pussy." There was no hairstyle that could convey, "My dick gets hard when a hot woman growls at me." It wasn't a fashion statement, for me or for them, but somehow, we found each other. Powered by the adrenaline rush of knowing I'd have a boy to test out the new red suede flogger I'd picked up at a sex shop that afternoon, I blazed my way through the set list and even added two songs to the encore.

"Hot damn!" Genius greeted us as we left the stage. "Someone's got a fan." He was onto me; he was always onto me, and not just because I'd pointed out Jacob earlier. Genius could spot these guys a mile away, too, and sometimes I was kind enough to let him play with the ones I didn't want, if they swung that way. He knew, though, that my music was powered by sexual desire, and that I was hungry to continue that flow of energy.

"Should I go get him for you?" The others just looked at us and rolled their eyes. They didn't quite share our groupie-spotting vision.

"Nah, make him wait a little while. Give him these to play with," I said, reaching under my short skirt to take off my sweaty panties.

I hopped in the shower, even though there's a part of me that likes the sticky post-show sensation, the way the heat and the glitter and the magic still cling to me. I emerged and slipped into another skirt, a very short latex one, skipping the panties. I slipped a see-through white tank top over my head, knowing my nipple piercings would be visible, and brushed my favorite permanent red lipstick back onto my lips. I smiled at myself in the mirror, reminding myself, as I do every day, how lucky I am to have crafted the perfect life for myself. If I'd been stuck in a house all day with a baby, even if I had a guitar by my side, I just wouldn't have been happy. I see the joy my friends get from their kids, on the rare occasions I get to visit with them, and know that, in its own way, rocking out makes me just as happy. As does what happens after.

I slipped into a pair of tall black heels, the kind I can't wear onstage lest I topple over. I don't need the height, but I love the way they make me feel, and they give me an advantage over even the tallest guy, though the ones I tend to select rarely top five ten. Something about being short must add to their inferiority complex, or simply their desire to submit. I added some apricot hand cream to my pulse points and cleavage and headed out. There was Jacob, pacing around the lobby. He looked almost startled to see me when I approached.

"Hi," he said, his eyes widening as he looked up at me.

"Let's go outside, I want a cigarette." I'm down to a few a day, and they are my treats. This one wasn't so much about nicotine as cementing our roles; I was the one acting, he was reacting. I was going to smoke, and Jacob was going to light my cigarette and simply watch me. I tugged him down the hallway and out the back door, then handed him my lighter and stuck the cigarette between my lips. I was impressed that he didn't fumble it, because I could tell he was nervous. The flame rose up and I touched the tip of the cigarette to it, then inhaled. I didn't ask if he wanted one, because I didn't care.

"How long have you been coming to my shows?"

"Since the first album. I was a fan right away."

"Favorite song?" I asked.

He paused, and I could tell he was really giving it some thought, not just scrambling to come up with a name because he wanted to spend some time with me. "'Pussy on Fire,'" he said. "Followed by 'Eat Me.'"

"Good choices," I said, then inhaled, before blowing smoke in his face. He didn't flinch; in fact, it almost looked like he stepped closer to me. "You're not a virgin, are you?" I asked.

"No, ma'am. But I've only been with three girls. And none of them were anything like you."

I smiled. "I wouldn't think they would be. I'm one of a kind. Can you handle me? Or rather, can I handle you? If you come backstage with me, I'm not going to go easy on you." With that, I grabbed his arm and raked my nails along his pale skin, watching the red lines rise. So many women with extra-long nails don't realize how sexy a weapon they can be.

"Yes," he said, his voice slightly strangled now, as if fighting to get out. "You can do anything you want with me. I'd like to be yours for the night."

"That's what I like to hear. I don't want you thinking there's a chance this can be more than a one-night thing; I don't work like that. I want to use your body and then I'll be gone tomorrow. Are you sure you're okay with that?" I asked, tossing my smoke on the sidewalk and grinding it out with a turn of my heel. Jacob's gaze ran from my shoe up my leg to my face.

"Definitely. I'd be honored for any time you'd like to spend with me."

"Very good. First I want to see your cock, though, make sure it's big enough." That wasn't strictly true; I'm really not a size queen, despite the rumors about me. Sure, a nine- or even ten-inch dick can feel amazing, but the truth is that some of my best lovers have been men with cocks on the smaller side. Maybe it's that they don't come with quite the baggage, the arrogance, of the big dicked; they seem to know their place and are very eager to please. But I did want to make Jacob work for the chance to be with me, to prove that he really was willing to risk something of himself, because otherwise, there were dozens just like him, and I could have my pick.

I wanted him, but I didn't want him to know that. "Show me. Show me right here. Unzip your jeans and let me see what I'm getting."

To his credit, Jacob didn't ask what I meant or try to wheedle me into stepping inside to have our big show and tell. He angled his body toward the building, almost like he was going to take a piss, and very quickly slid his zipper down and took his dick out of what I thought were a pair of blue briefs. He held it in his hand and it looked impressive indeed, long and firm. I felt a twitch, imagining it inside me. I've been told I think "like a guy," because just the sight of a well-hung cock can be all it takes to make me wet. I don't care if that's a supposedly masculine trait or what, I'm happy to be the kind of woman who likes uncompli- cated sex, who's knows exactly what she wants and goes for it.

"That'll do," is what I told Jacob. He smiled and tucked his dick back in his pants. I debated for a second between a back- stage fuck and taking him to my hotel room; backstage isn't exactly the lap of luxury, but it has its charms, especially when I want to put a guy through his paces. It's a little hard to act like I'm torturing a man in a five-star hotel, but then again, the record company was paying my keep, so why not take advan- tage of their largess?

"Stay right here," I said, leaving Jacob outside in the cold while I went to grab my purse.

"Don't stay up too late, Gina," Genius warned me, and I gave him the finger.

I ran back outside, smiling at the hubbub of New York all around. I do love being onstage, but the afterglow of a fabulous show is where I really shine, when I have no obligations for at least ten hours and an entire night's worth of thrills lay before me. I pulled Jacob close for a kiss, inching my hand down his pants. His ass was on the flat side, but I liked holding it, especially when I felt him react, his breath coming faster.

I hailed us a cab, even though we could've taken a limo. I was in a hurry and I wasn't in this to show off. I wanted Jacob to be impressed with me, not the trappings of fame. Once in the cab, I pulled out a spare piece of purple bondage rope I keep in my purse (even rock stars should be prepared for anything!) and told Jacob to give me his wrists. I could practically hear the "What about my seat belt?" query dying on his lips. He turned and thrust his wrists back at me, and, knowing the cab driver was watching, I expertly cinched them together.

Then I had my captive turn and make small talk with me, as if this were any other evening. In only a few minutes we were at the hotel. I tipped the driver generously, then helped Jacob out of the taxi. I'd have to undo his wrists later to get him naked, but the idea of making him walk with purple rope around his wrists charmed me.

A doorman ushered us inside and onto our own private elevator, where I made Jacob twirl around for the security cameras. "Get down on your knees and put your hands up like you're a puppy." I'm not that into role-play, generally, but something about the situation, and Jacob's expression when the words left my lips, made me glad I'd said it. Pushing a sub almost to the point of discomfort, resting on that delicate, tantalizing edge, is what I like best about playing. I have to be able to read people fast, because I don't get that long to enjoy them.

Jacob sank to his knees and even gave me the added touch of sticking his tongue out and panting. "Are you good with your tongue, Jacob?" I asked, grabbing it between my fingers and pinching lightly.

"Yes, ma'am." I granted him a smile, then shoved him backward and kissed him hungrily, knowing my lipstick would smear all over his face. Then I nudged him with my shoe's pointy tip. "Get up."

He stood and I dragged him by the shirt collar to my room. "I want to see how fast you can make me come with that tongue of yours." When I was younger, I was more like Jacob—eager to please and hungry; very, very hungry; for cock, pussy, dildos, whatever. I couldn't get enough of going down. These days, I've discovered that, with the right guys, the ones who'll do anything for me, getting head can be even better than the best night spent on my knees. I stripped off my skirt and presented my pussy to Jacob, not for inspection, but to make sure he properly appreciated what he was getting.

"I like it a little rough," I said. "Not painful, but no gentle licking. Get in there good; use your tongue like a cock." I didn't need to say more; he was ready, willing and more than able. Jacob didn't care that I was tall enough to hover over him while he sat on the floor on his knees; this wasn't about his comfort, but my pleasure. I could tell he wanted to give me a fond farewell, to stand out from the other cute nerdy boys I'd pick up on tour. His mouth sucked me the way I'd asked, yet was also tender, and I watched him get lost in my cunt, savoring every second I granted him. I tugged on his hair, pulling him deeper, and felt him straining to get his tongue as far inside me as he could.

"Suck my clit now, and put three fingers inside me." I didn't have time to wonder what Jacob was thinking, but I could tell from the way he was moving beneath me that he was enjoying himself—maybe not as much as I was, but close enough. He immediately inserted his fingers and sucked my clit in a way that almost made me cry it was so good. "Yeah, like that," I breathed, my fingers loosening in his silky-soft hair as the tremors rose up in me. I melted into his tongue, his touch, and let out all the passion that had been building from the show's first note until now. I mashed my pussy into Jacob's face as he diligently licked me until I released him.

"Now bend over," I said, "and close your eyes." I grabbed the new flogger out of its bag, testing it against my hand before bringing it down on his upper back, loving the way the hit reverberated back into my arm. I find giving a flogging therapeutic, and from the noises Jacob was making, it seemed like he did too. I whacked his back till it was bright red, then moved on to his ass, giving it a few solid strokes that I knew would sting the next day.

"Now draw me a bath," I said. "Use the bath gel that's next to the tub, and make it hot." I checked my voice mail messages while Jacob ran the water. When I was ready, I grabbed my cigarettes and sank into the tub. "Light this one for me."

Jacob did, and I sat there smoking, while he perched on the toilet seat, uncertain about what would happen next. "Get my phone; I want to take a souvenir photo of your cock." Jacob leapt up to get it, then took off his pants when I told him to. I made him stroke it for me, holding it so as to make it look as long as possible. "Now jerk off for me, give me a little show. I'm gonna tape it, but don't worry—I won't show anyone else." As I relaxed into the warmth of the bubbles, inhaling my final daily allotment of nicotine, and watched a young man I'd never see again give me my own private sex show, I thought, *Life is good. Damn good. Being a rock star certainly has its privileges.* I even let Jacob come on my tits as a reward, because I'm nice like that. Then I sent him on his way, tucked my warm, naked body between the sheets and slept like a baby.

ABOUT THE AUTHORS

ABBY ABBOT (a pseudonym) resides with her (outwardly) more respectable alter ego in the United Kingdom. She turns her writing hand to a variety of genres with equally varied success, but thinks it's wonderful how often writing dirty inspires her to get up and do the real deal.

CHRISSIE BENTLEY (chrissiebentley.wordpress.com) is the author of nine erotic novels and novellas, including the steamy-punk detective trilogy *Ambrose Horne,* and the BDSM scorcher *Miss America.* In addition, her short fiction has appeared in a multitude of anthologies, including *Best Women's Erotica 2011.*

DANIEL BURNELL's erotic stories and novellas have been or will soon be published by *Mainstream Erotica, Fishnet Magazine, For The Girls, Etopia Press, The Erotic Woman* and in anthologies from Cleis Press, Lyrotica and Coming Together, among other places.

RACHEL KRAMER BUSSEL (rachelkramerbussel.com) is a New York-based author, editor, blogger and event organizer;

editor of over forty anthologies, including *Obsessed; Gotta Have It; The Mile High Club; Peep Show; Orgasmic; Fast Girls; Spanked; Bottoms Up; Please, Sir; Please, Ma'am; Best Bondage Erotica 2011* and *2012,* and is *Best Sex Writing* series editor.

HEIDI CHAMPA (heidichampa.blogspot.com) has been published in *Best Women's Erotica 2010, Playing with Fire, Frenzy* and *Ultimate Curves.* She has also steamed up the pages of *Bust Magazine.* If you prefer your erotica in electronic form, she can be found at Clean Sheets, Ravenous Romance, Oysters and Chocolate and The Erotic Woman.

LILY K. CHO is a fortysomething, suburban working mom. She lives in the San Francisco Bay Area and, after reading erotica for the last twenty-five years, has finally decided to start writing it too.

JAN DARBY is a lawyer and a storyteller, writing legal documents by day and erotic romance by night. She has a story in another Cleis Press anthology, *Sweet Love: Erotic Fantasies for Couples,* and has had several short stories and novellas published electronically.

MAY DEVA (maydeva.wordpress.com) has been published in *Kinkyville: Thirteen More Stories of Small Town Naughty,* and in hearteater, a creative collaboration sprung from Twitter. May participated in Alison Tyler's Smut Marathon, a ten month project which featured fifteen writers. Her story, "Subway Subterfuge," won the competition.

EMERALD (thegreenlightdistrict.org) has had erotic fiction published in anthologies edited by Violet Blue, Rachel Kramer

Bussel, and Kristina Wright, among others, as well as at various erotic websites.

I. G. FREDERICK's stories have appeared in *Hustler Fantasies, Forum, Foreplay* and several print anthologies. She currently also has short stories available for electronic download, including "If You Love Someone," named one of the top ten romance short stories by the Preditors & Editors readers poll.

CYNTHIA HAMILTON (cynthiahamilton.net) is the pen name of a bisexual woman living in San Francisco. By day, she edits fiction professionally. After hours, she likes to let her own imagination off the leash.

KEV HENLEY has published three science fiction novellas: *COB, Sperm Count* and *Polar Opposites*. Kev has dabbled in much darker territory with his recently released thriller, *Lichess*, and when time permits, he brings his historical and fantasy works-in-progress off the back burner.

D. L. KING (dlkingerotica.blogspot.com) is a smut writing-and editing New Yorker: editor of the Lambda Literary Award Finalist, *Where the Girls Are*, as well as *The Sweetest Kiss, Spank* and *Carnal Machines*, and the author of two novels of female domination and male submission, *The Melinoe Project* and *The Art of Melinoe*.

N. T. MORLEY is the author of the novels of dominance and submission *The Parlor, The Limousine, The Circle, The Appointment, The Victor, The Dancer, The Adulteress*, and the trilogies *The Library, The Office* and *The Castle*, as well as the short story collections *In a Stranger's Hands* and *Taking Dictation*.

THOMAS S. ROCHE's (Thomasroche.com) debut novel is *The Panama Laugh*. His prior books include *In the Shadow of the Gargoyle* and *Graven Images*, edited with Nancy Kilpatrick; *Sons of Darkness* and *Brothers of the Night*, edited with Michael Rowe; and two short-story collections, *Dark Matter* and *Parts of Heaven*.

AUSTIN STEVENS is the pseudonym of a very naughty author who lurks in online forums and has really dirty thoughts.

DONNA GEORGE STOREY (DonnaGeorgeStorey.com) is the author of *Amorous Woman*, a semiautobiographical tale of an American woman's love affair with Japan. Her short fiction has appeared in numerous journals and anthologies including, *Best Women's Erotica*, *Women in Lust*, *Best American Erotica*, *The Mammoth Book of Best New Erotica* and *Penthouse*.

ALISON TYLER's (alisontyler.com) sultry short stories have appeared in more than one hundred anthologies including *Sex for America*, *Liaisons* and *Best Women's Erotica 2011*. She is the editor of over fifty erotic anthologies and twenty-five novels, including *Tiffany Twisted*, *Melt With You* and *Something About Workmen*.

KRISTINA WRIGHT (kristinawright.com) is a full-time writer and the editor of the Cleis Press anthologies *Fairy Tale Lust*, *Dream Lover*, *Steamlust* and *Best Erotic Romance 2012*. Kristina's erotica and erotic romance fiction has appeared in over eighty print anthologies. She is living and writing happily ever after in Virginia with her family.

ABOUT
THE EDITOR

VIOLET BLUE (tinynibbles.com, @violetblue) is a CBSi/ZDNet columnist, a *Forbes* "Web Celeb" and one of *Wired*'s "Faces of Innovation"—in addition to being a blogger, high-profile tech personality and podcaster. Violet has nearly forty award-winning, best-selling books; an excerpt from her *Smart Girl's Guide to Porn* is featured on Oprah Winfrey's website. She is regarded as the foremost expert in the field of sex and technology, a sex-positive pundit in mainstream media (CNN, "The Oprah Winfrey Show," "The Tyra Banks Show") and is regularly interviewed, quoted and featured prominently by major media outlets. Blue also writes for media outlets such as *MacLife, O: The Oprah Magazine* and the UN-sponsored international health organization RH Reality Check. She headlines at conferences ranging from ETech, LeWeb and SXSW: Interactive, to Google Tech Talks at Google, Inc. The *London Times* named Blue "one of the 40 bloggers who really count."

More Women's Erotica from Violet Blue

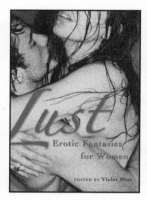

Lust
Erotic Fantasies for Women
Edited by Violet Blue

Lust is a collection of erotica by and for women, a fierce and joyous celebration of female desire and the triple-X trouble it gets us into.
ISBN 978-1-57344-280-0 $14.95

Best Women's Erotica 2011
Edited by Violet Blue

"Every single story is layered top to toe with explicit sex—hard and wet and mean and sweet, flowing with love and fused with characters who finally feel like us, with no apologies..." —from the Introduction
ISBN 978-1-57344-423-1 $15.95

Best of Best Women's Erotica 2
Edited by Violet Blue

Lovingly handpicked by Violet Blue, those erotic gems have been polished to perfection by the bestselling editor in women's erotica.
ISBN 978-1-57344-379-1 $15.95

Girls on Top
Explicit Erotica for Women
Edited by Violet Blue

"If you enjoy sexy stories about women with desirable minds (and bodies and libidos that match) then *Girls on Top* needs to be on your reading list."—Erotica Readers and Writers Association
ISBN 978-1-57344-340-1 $14.95

Lips Like Sugar
Edited by Violet Blue

Sure to keep you up past bedtime, the stories in *Lips Like Sugar* will arouse your appetite for something truly sweet.
ISBN 978-1-57344-232-9 $14.95

Best Erotica Series

"Gets racier every year."—*San Francisco Bay Guardian*

Ordering is easy! Call us toll free or fax us to place your MC/VISA order.
You can also mail the order form below with payment to:
Cleis Press, 2246 Sixth St., Berkeley, CA 94710.

ORDER FORM

QTY	TITLE	PRICE
_____	_____	_____
_____	_____	_____
_____	_____	_____
_____	_____	_____
_____	_____	_____
_____	_____	_____
_____	_____	_____
_____	_____	_____

SUBTOTAL _____

SHIPPING _____

SALES TAX _____

TOTAL _____

Add $3.95 postage/handling for the first book ordered and $1.00 for each additional book. Outside North America, please contact us for shipping rates. California residents add 8.75% sales tax. Payment in U.S. dollars only.

* Free book of equal or lesser value. Shipping and applicable sales tax extra.

Cleis Press • Phone: (800) 780-2279 • Fax: (510) 845-8001
orders@cleispress.com • www.cleispress.com
You'll find more great books on our website

Follow us on Twitter @cleispress • Friend/fan us on Facebook